there will never

be another night

like this

JOHN SALTER

there will never be another night like this

STORIES

SLANT
BOOKS

THERE WILL NEVER BE ANOTHER NIGHT LIKE THIS
Stories

Slant Books
P.O. Box 60295
Seattle, WA 98160

www.slantbooks.org

Cataloguing-in-Publication data:

Names: Salter, John.

Title: There will never be another night like this : stories / John Salter.

Description: Seattle, WA: Slant Books, 2024

Identifiers: ISBN 978-1-63982-154-9 (hardcover) | ISBN 978-1-63982-153-2 (paperback) | ISBN 978-1-63982-155-6 (ebook)

Subjects: LCSH: Short stories | Short stories, American | North Dakota--Fiction | Minnesota--Fiction

For William Borden

1938-2010

teacher, friend, brother

Contents

A New Science

SOME KIND OF COMIC BOOK convention is being held in one of the banquet rooms at the hotel. Barker just wants a gin and tonic, but the lounge is crowded with geeks carrying their loot, comic books and stickers and buttons, trading their loot, spreading their loot on the bar. He feels like an outcast when he squeezes his way between them. The geeks are harassing the bartender, ordering complicated drinks, *Sex on the Beach* and *Cum in a Hot Tub*, *Liquid Viagra*, college drinks like that, even though the geeks all appear to be approaching middle age. The bartender spots Barker, aims her finger at him like a pistol. Cups her other hand behind her ear and furrows her brow.

"Gin and tonic," he shouts.

The bartender makes it right away, serves him first. For this, Barker gives her a two dollar tip. Barker intends to have more than one gin and tonic and doesn't want to have to wait.

He takes a sip. It is everything he dreamed of when he got dressed and slipped out of the room, rode twenty floors down in the elevator. The elevator ceiling was mirrored, and Barker tilted his head back to straighten his hair until it occurred to him they probably had a security camera up there, that some fat-ass in a utility room was probably making fun of him. So he quit that, decided instead to find a bathroom on the first floor to freshen up in, but he really needed that gin and tonic. He's not an alcoholic, goes weeks between drinks, has a bottle of Wild Turkey—unopened—that's been in the cupboard for years. A gift from his brother in Nebraska, and every time Louis stops by, he asks if the bottle is open yet, and Barker offers to open it on the spot, but Louis holds up his hands and says no, not on his account. And Barker always thinks he'll open it when Louis mentions he's coming up north, but of course, he never remembers. An alcoholic, Barker thinks, wouldn't have a dusty bottle of Wild Turkey, but he *was* fixed on getting the gin and tonic. And when he stepped from the elevator and checked the map to make sure he was correct about where the bar was, and then saw it was full of geeks, he panicked. Got it in his head that all the gin would be gone, the bottles piled in a garbage can, and decided he looked good enough for a hotel bar.

He drinks the first one too fast, waves for another, lights a cigarette. The geek next to him makes a show of waving away the smoke. Barker pretends he doesn't notice. He studies his coaster.

The woman upstairs, in his room, his bed. The tall woman. The way she fell asleep afterward reminds Barker of the deer he killed when he was fifteen. After he shot the deer, it ran. Barker was on his way back to the camper, sleepy and looking forward to shucking his coveralls and taking a nap. His father had gotten him up early, and at the edge of the clearing where they'd parked the camper, in the predawn, they'd split up, going to the tree stands they'd hung days before. Then: endless waiting, trying to stay awake, watching the trail below. No deer had shown up. Barker was on his way in when the deer, the buck, ran across the trail in front of him and stopped fifteen yards into the trees. Looked back, not at Barker but in the direction of his father's stand. Barker had been a little relieved to see no deer, but here was a buck, and he shot it. Raised the old Savage 99 lever-action and shot the buck. It didn't fall all the way over, just stumbled, regained its footing, and ran. Didn't get very far, and when Barker caught up to the buck, it was on the ground, fighting death, kicking and bucking wildly, and then it died. Died fighting death right to the end.

That was how she fell asleep. Bucked and kicked and moaned and then passed out. The tall woman. In his bed, upstairs.

The geeks on his left are doing shots now. Tequila. One of them leans over to Barker. "Hey, aren't you the Captain America guy?"

"Say again?"

"Aren't you a vendor?"

"No."

His new gin and tonic shows up. There is gin running down the outside of the glass. That's how crazy it is for the bartender, how busy she is. She takes Barker's money, blows loose hair from her eyes. "Keep it," he says.

She smiles. The geek who hates smoke pays for his beer with exact change, folds his wallet up, tucks it back into his pocket. It strikes Barker that two kinds of people live on the planet. Those who tip and those who stiff. Barker always tips extra. Bartenders, waitresses, the Vietnamese woman who cuts his hair back home in Fargo. His wife waited tables when he met her. He used to go for dinner after work, eat and read, then drink coffee and read. She got to know his habits. He always dropped an ice cube into his coffee to cool it off. She started doing that for him when she brought his coffee. Little things like that. Never brought him grape jelly with his toast after he told her how all he ever got growing up was grape jelly.

He lights another smoke. Again, much flailing from the geek. The geek has a stack of comic books in plastic sleeves. He has his hands at his sides, and he bends to study the top comic book cover. He studies it for such a long time that Barker wonders if the geek is falling asleep. But then he lifts the comic book and tucks it beneath the others and begins to study the next cover. Laughter erupts among the tequila geeks. One of them tried to drink a shot without using his hands and spilled the shot down his shirt. The geek is in his thirties with glasses and a cell phone clipped to his belt. They are all in their thirties with glasses and cell phones clipped to their belts. "Cut him off, cut him off," they shout at the bartender. They want to engage her. They want to draw her in, but she's too busy. Barker doubts she would give them the time of day even if she weren't busy. She looks a little jaded. She wipes down the counter and cracks only a perfunctory smile before flitting away.

The woman in his bed is not his wife. His wife is in their bed, he thinks. No, he doesn't just think she is. He knows she is. She is in their bed in Fargo, probably sleeping, with the remote in her hand. If the remote is not in her hand, it is probably just a few inches from her hand, on the smooth green sheet. From the ceiling it would look a bit like a crime scene photograph but with a remote control by her hand and not a revolver. If tomorrow evening he got on the train and rolled west through the night with his head against the window, watching small towns flick by, the occasional farmhouse light, drifting in and out of sleep, if he got off the train in downtown Fargo and climbed into his Oldsmobile, drove home, hit the garage door button when he turned the corner so the door would be open by the time he reached the driveway, if he pulled in and parked next to his wife's Cavalier, got out with his suitcase, shut the door, went into the dark kitchen, if he petted the cat and drank a glass of water and took a leak, brushed his teeth or maybe not, if he went into the bedroom and took off his clothes by the light of the television, if he crawled into bed with his wife, he might not notice right away if it was a revolver by her hand and not the remote.

He fishes a chunk of lime from his glass and chews it, glances around and swallows it. His wife has never talked about killing herself, so this whole business with the remote control and the revolver is just nonsense, he decides, the kind of garbage you consider while drinking a gin and tonic in a hotel bar. His wife is not depressed. Isn't happy in the ecstatic sense. Nobody is. On a scale of one to ten with one being very unhappy and ten being overjoyed, he would place his wife at a seven. Six. Six isn't bad, overall. Even five is okay. He means generally, in the big scheme of things, not five as a snapshot of a given moment. Like the tequila geeks, he decides. Tonight, they're sitting at eight or nine. And the bartender. She could be at two or three. Tomorrow morning the reverse could be true.

He orders another gin and tonic. He isn't drunk. They are weak drinks at this hotel. The rooms are small, too, smaller than you'd think looking at the hotel from the sidewalk. She—the woman upstairs—said, "Fargo? Where are you staying?" And he said the Hyatt Regency. And she laughed and pointed. Pointed up, and there it was. He wasn't really lost. That was the thing. He had finished his business and bought a cup of gourmet coffee and did some window shopping. Then he ate a meatball sandwich and read *City Pages*. And he was walking back to the hotel to call his wife and fill her in, watch some television, go to bed, when he saw her on the sidewalk. She was smoking a cigarette and walking in tight circles. She was tall and wore thick-soled shoes that made her look even taller. And she was wearing a short dress that made her legs look longer. And she had meaty legs, not spindly legs. Haunchy? Was that the word? "Listen," he said, when one of her tight circles brought her around to face him. "Can you tell a hick from Fargo, North Dakota, how to get back to his hotel?"

The smoke-hating geek is joined by a girl with jewel-encrusted glasses and a high, shiny forehead. She drops a giant jumble of keys onto the bar. The keys spread out into something resembling a metal tarantula. She is out of breath. "Okay," she says. "I told Larry that Cassie had too much to drink, so I'm driving her home. I said I might just crash at her place, so he shouldn't wait up."

"Cool. We'll have one more and then go."

The girl catches Barker looking at her. She stares at him for a moment. "Who is this guy?" she says to the geek.

"I don't know. His smoke is pissing me off, though."

"Let's move."

"No. I have a right to sit here. More of a right than he has."

They are talking as if Barker is deaf. Or as if he doesn't speak English. And it is plain English, not jargon, not slang, not words he might not be familiar with, like when the tall woman said, "One of my clients just gave me some kick-ass chronic."

"Chronic?"

"Kick ass. He's a drummer."

He tried again. "Client?"

She jerked her thumb behind her. They were standing in front of a salon. Barker hadn't noticed. He went over and cupped his hands to the window and peeked inside, saw two women in black smocks on a sofa, reading magazines.

"I'm off," she said. "I don't even work on Fridays, but he has this gig tonight in St. Cloud. And I'm like, it'll cost you. So he hooked me up. Why do you keep staring at my legs?"

"I like those shoes."

She laughed and covered his eyes with her palm. Her palm was warm. "What color are they?"

"Black," he said.

"Okay," she said. "These are fucking Wal-Mart shoes. Bet you couldn't tell."

He shook his head.

"So anyway, Fargo. Mr. Fargo. Sounds like one of those dumb radio shows. Fred Fargo, Park Ranger."

"That's me."

"So I want to fire up this kick ass you-know-what. And you have a room right up there."

"Isn't that something?"

"Can you do the math?"

"I can."

The tequila geeks have gotten kind of somber. They are reminiscing about comic books they owned in their youth, comics lost or traded or ripped or rolled into flyswatters. This morphs into recollection about toys that, had the geeks saved them, would be worth real money, G.I. Joes and certain Star Wars figures, battery-powered baby dolls, Matchbox cars. Lionel trains. Had they saved everything, they'd all be rich. One of the geeks slaps his palm against the bar and says, philosophically, "It's *because* nobody saved them that they're worth so much now. If everyone had saved stuff, it would be worthless."

It's a good point, Barker thinks. A simple argument. Simple is often best. His lawyer told him that, earlier in the day, a couple hours before he met the tall woman. Barker is suing a trucking company for the accident that left his son Kevin in a "vegetative state." His son's car had broken down, it was on the shoulder, and Kevin was opening the hood, probably to check the serpentine belt, the belt that in newer cars seems to control everything—controls too much, if you ask Barker—when the semi hit the car and trapped Kevin underneath it. Dragged him underneath it. The trucking company is a national outfit, and the suit is, in Barker's opinion, beyond the abilities of Fargo attorneys. For this project, Barker wants someone who might be considered "high-powered" now and then. So he came down to Minneapolis with the Kevin file. And he took the Amtrak because, ever since the accident, he had trouble driving on highways. If he saw a semi in the rear-view mirror, his heart would race, and he'd feel like he was choking. He wondered if he should tell the lawyer about this but decided against it because he wants this to be about Kevin, not him. The lawyer looked like a lawyer should look in Barker's estimation—graying at the temples, handsome, like an airline pilot, actually. His secretary served Barker ice water with a lemon slice and spoke in a hushed, respectful tone. The lawyer said, "I know exactly how to handle these people, Mr. Barker," no less than three times. The meeting only took an hour. It takes longer than that to feed Kevin now, who is in a special home in Bemidji, with a lush view of trees and a lake, loons and deer, a view that probably means nothing to Kevin.

He sighs, lights another cigarette. This time he glares at the smoke-hating geek. He uses a trick he's learned over the past year, and that is to think of his son, the trucking company, the catheter bag silently filling with urine, the cardboard box that arrived from Hamline University with Kevin's belongings, still unopened and gathering dust on Barker's workbench in the garage. He collects all these images in his head and focuses them into a stare, like catching the sun in a magnifying glass, and it works, the geek turns away without saying a word and studies his comic books.

He orders a fourth gin and tonic. Or is it his fifth? He doesn't know. It doesn't matter. Like it didn't matter, the tall woman said, when he asked if she wanted a bottled water from the mini bar or an imported beer. On the elevator, she squeezed his cheeks with her fingers, shaping his lips into fish lips, the sort of thing you'd do to a child. In the room, after snooping around a bit, opening drawers and the closet door, she sat at the small table by the window, kicked off her shoes, and lighted the joint. Barker couldn't open the window; they didn't open, probably to prevent suicides or accidents, and he stopped short of turning on the bathroom fan because it struck him that someone on another floor might smell the marijuana coming through the ventilation shaft and call security. So he smoked three cigarettes in a row to mask the smell while she smoked the joint, which burned more slowly than the cigarettes with their chemical additives. She offered him the joint, and he took one drag to be polite and waved it off the next time. When she was finished, she took one of his cigarettes, drank some Perrier, and stared at him for the longest time.

What was he thinking before? His wife isn't at a six on the happiness scale. She might have been for years but not since Kevin's accident. The scale no longer applied. A different kind of scale was in order. A sub-scale, a misery index. Now she says things like, "I don't know if I can bear it." And: "If I thought I could forget all of this by dying, then

I'd want to die." But other days, she wakes up early and sits at Kevin's computer, posting messages on a brain injury bulletin board, some kind of electronic support group. She calls someone named Randy on the phone once or twice a week. Randy's son is in the same home as Kevin. His son had dived into shallow water and struck his head on a submerged railroad tie. There is nobody to sue. Randy is working two jobs to keep his son in the home. There is no way he can even begin to think about bringing his son home, hiring the necessary help, performing the necessary modifications to the house like Barker and his wife are planning to do. Lately, Barker's wife has been hinting about giving Randy some money if the lawsuit pans out. Not asking Barker but hinting. Now Barker thinks, why not? Why not lay a couple hundred thousand on Randy? But he isn't sure if it is guilt driving the thought, or the gin, or something else entirely.

The tall woman said, "I get horny sometimes when I smoke weed. Sometimes I get hungry, sometimes I get horny. Sometimes I get all fucking paranoid."

"It's the enzymes," Barker explained. "Different plant varieties have different enzymes."

"What are you, some kind of drug expert?"

"I'm an agronomist."

"What's that?"

"I'm a plant scientist," he said. "I study soil and plants. How they work together." It was how he explained it to everyone not of an agricultural background, auto mechanics and store clerks. How he had explained it to Kevin when he was old enough to realize different fathers had different jobs.

The tall woman went to the window, leaned against the glass. "If we were on the other side, I could see Oleander."

"Oleander?"

"My salon."

He stood right behind her, not sure how to proceed. Still not sure if she had come up for more than the marijuana. This was a new science, like cloning. He was inches from her. Then she turned new science into old by pressing her bottom against him. He unzipped her dress and yanked it down. Kissed her broad shoulders, squeezed her rear, rubbed against her. She turned around and kind of danced him to the bed in her bra and panties. He undressed and sat on the tight spread. His pale skin seemed to glow. She pushed him down and sat on him. They did some things he had only heard about. He wasn't sure whether he liked doing them. Then they did some more familiar things, with her on top, then Barker on top, between her muscular legs. And she sort of went crazy toward the end, raising her hips, lifting Barker into the air, and she bit his chin, and then she fell asleep, reminding him of the deer, how it went crazy right before it died. He cleaned up a little, smoked a cigarette by the window, drank from the Perrier, wiping the bottle mouth first before realizing how idiotic that was, considering what they'd been doing. That's when he started craving a gin and tonic. But he sat for half an hour, watching her sleep, watching the city lights spreading wildly, before dressing and leaving the room.

"One more?" the bartender asks.

Barker nods. The smoke-hating geek is kissing his girlfriend, mistress, whatever she is, they're kissing. The tequila geeks are exchanging email addresses, phone numbers, punching the information into their phones. He wonders if the tall woman is awake, if she's gone, if she'll be there until morning. He has no preference. He can't remember her name or even if she told him her name. He didn't tell her his name. That kind of conversation might have come after the sex, like in the movies, stretched out on the bed, sharing a cigarette. Not that he wanted that, but afterwards would have been the appropriate time. But she went a little crazy and passed out.

He's a bit tipsy and stumbles a little when he gets off the barstool. Not much but he bumps into one of the tequila geeks. "Sorry," he says, and the tequila geek ignores him. As Barker leaves, the smoke-hating geek leans across to the tequila geek. "Is that the Captain America dude?"

"No."

"Who is he?"

Barker slows, curious about what the answer will be. Then he changes his mind and tries to hurry away. He isn't fast enough.

"Just some loser."

"That's what we thought, but he kind of looks like the Captain America guy."

"He's like the total opposite of that guy."

Out in the lobby, Barker tries to retrace his steps to the elevator. He remembers something his father told him on that hunting trip when he was fifteen, how he should stop and look back every few yards so he'd recognize the trail on the way back. Not enough people did that, his father said. Now Barker studies the long red carpeted hall. What if things look the same both ways? He is too tired to wrap his mind around something like this, so he just wanders until he finds the elevator. He pushes the button, the doors open right away, and he is going up, then, quickly and silently.

He is quiet entering the room, but the lights are on, and she is gone. He surveys the room and wonders vaguely if she took anything. There wasn't much to take. Just his small suitcase and the brown accordion folder containing the Kevin file. At the attorney's office, the secretary had slipped away to copy everything—the Highway Patrol reports, doctor's reports, insurance company letters, photographs, even Kevin's college transcripts. She had copied everything, and when she came back, she set the accordion folder on the floor next to Barker's chair, and when he looked down her hand was drawing away from the file, and there was something about her pale hand and sculpted but unpainted nails, lingering a moment on the folder, something small and touching, that made him feel both appreciative and patronized at the same time.

He undresses, turns on the television, watches a few minutes of Jay Leno's monologue. His wife may be watching Jay Leno also. Maybe Randy is watching, too, getting ready for his graveyard shift at a gas station. And it is possible but not probable that Kevin is watching Jay Leno, if one of the nurses has it on, maybe has it on in every room so she can catch bits and pieces of the show as she makes her rounds. He looks over at the bed, the spread rolled back, the sheets rumpled. His father showed him shallow depressions in the pine needles where deer slept during the day. Barker thinks he sees the tall woman's outline on the sheet but isn't sure. He goes over and presses his hand against the sheet to see if it is warm. It is, but he can't tell if it is normal warm or warm because she was there recently. He stretches out and laces his fingers behind his head. The deer didn't go down quietly, like he had imagined it would, dropping instantly, lying in repose as the sun brightened the new day enough for a photograph with Dad's ancient Argus camera. It fought death pretty hard—or maybe it didn't after all, he thinks. Maybe it fought off whatever *life* remained in it because it somehow knew life was going to take a bad turn. Maybe that was what the buck was doing when it kicked and grunted and rolled. Maybe that was the smart thing to do. He thinks of his son, with a bandanna perennially around his neck for the staff to use to wipe drool from his chin, thinks of his wife always on the lookout for interesting bandannas, Minnesota Viking bandannas, bandannas with little black Scottish terriers around the border, and he gets out of bed, pulls on his pants, his shirt, plugs his bare feet into his shoes. He thinks about hurling himself through the window but opens the door and heads back down to the bar instead.

Habitats

BACK IN IOWA, HIS PARENTS had never entertained, but now it seemed like every few weeks, people from his father's office would show up on a Friday afternoon. His father worked for the Diocese of Rochester, something to do with human relations, social justice, Nils wasn't quite sure, but they helped those in need. His father worked alongside priests, nuns, and some regular people who wanted to improve the world. They all drank a lot. In Iowa, there had never been any liquor in the house, but now there was quite a bar assembled in the space under the window seat below the bay window in the dining room, bottles of gin, bourbon, vodka, various mixes. Nils had gotten into the booze one night when his parents were gone, encouraged by his older sister, and sampled everything until he was hammered, on his bed, the room spinning. When his parents came home, they were alarmed but not overly so, because they had gone through the same thing with his sister and saw it as more or less inevitable. His father had said he would not be punished because the terrible hangover that awaited him would be punishment enough. But in the morning, Nils felt great and came down the stairs for breakfast cheerfully. His father had seemed disappointed but kept his word and did not punish him. He did make Nils promise not to take any more booze from the cabinet. Nils had noted that he wasn't asked not to drink any more booze *in general*, and so he agreed. And so far, he had kept his promise and stayed out of the liquor cabinet, largely because he had grown to prefer beer over the hard stuff, and his parents rarely had beer on hand in between their gatherings.

This morning, his mother was cranky because people were coming over again in the afternoon, and the house was a mess, and nobody was helping her. She lighted one menthol from the butt of another in the middle of complaining about it. They were living in the biggest house they'd ever lived in, a stately home on Birr Street, with five bedrooms, a full dining room, a finished basement, a large pantry, all kinds of nooks and features. Nils and his brother were finally able to have their own rooms after sharing in Iowa, and before that, in Chicago. There was an above-ground swimming pool in the back yard, as yet unfilled because his parents saw it as a death trap, but it featured a huge deck on which his sister and her friends liked to hang out, reclining in chaise lounges, listening to the radio and flicking their cigarette butts into the rainwater that had collected at the bottom of the pool.

But more room meant more opportunity for clutter, more sur-faces begging for the dust rag. They'd never been known for keep-ing a spotless house, and it had not really mattered, with few people outside the family ever seeing how they lived. The people his father worked with all seemed to be pretty easygoing, not concerned with a little dust on the lampshade or cat hair on the back of the sofa, but his mother started in, marched up the stairs to wake his sister, and the house filled with tension like a balloon inflating. He didn't like to see his mother so upset. She was getting upset more and more often lately. She had never gotten that upset in Iowa. Nils shook open a big green garbage bag and roamed around, emptying ashtrays, getting rid of old newspapers, using a magazine subscription card to pry up a cat turd. His little brother angrily pushed around the vacuum cleaner, battering it against the furniture. His sister finally came down. She surveyed the activity and said, loud enough to be heard over the vac-uum cleaner, "Mother, what do you want me to do with your blanket and pillow since the living room is obviously your *bedroom* now?"

Their mother had taken to sleeping on the sofa, and they had sensed it wasn't something they should ask about, but here was Marie, bringing it up in her most sarcastic tone of voice. Nils was shocked, and his little brother aimed the Hoover in the other direction and hurried away. Their mother's face went sad, and his sister seemed to regret the comment. She didn't apologize, but she gathered up the bedding and said she'd just put it into the coat closet for now before slipping off to the kitchen and starting in on the dishes. It was all surface cleaning; nobody went much further, nobody washed the windows or mopped the kitchen floor, but it seemed to calm his mother enough so that when he said he was leaving to hang out with his friends, she did not object, just repeated that family mantra, *be careful.*

He went to Mary's Delicatessen and bought a pack of cigarettes and a Pepsi. For a while, Nils had gone through the popular charade of claiming he was buying cigarettes for his mother, trying to look like an innocent kid running an errand, until he realized the people at the store didn't care. Now he just asked for his Marlboros like everyone else, and the clerk slapped them onto the counter. He went outside and sat on the concrete ledge by the end of the building and waited for Mark to show up. They had not set a time more specific than mid-morning, so Nils didn't know how long he'd have to wait, but he didn't mind waiting. He was happy to be out of the house. From his perch, he could watch the cars flowing down Dewey Avenue, check out the people going in and out of the store. He sipped his Pepsi and smoked a cigarette, keeping it down by his side. Then he heard his name and turned, and Mark was coming down the sidewalk, bopping sort of like John Travolta carrying that paint can at the beginning of *Saturday Night Fever*. The movie, along with *Rocky*, had made Nils jealous that he wasn't Italian like Mark was, like so many of their classmates were. Nils thought his last name, *Larsen*, stacked against the names of his friends, *Alfieri, Furia, Montesano, Viscomi*, was colorless, common, devoid of history. Nils was Norwegian, Swedish, Mohawk, Abenaki, Scotch, and more, but when he had asked his father if they might have a little Italian in the mix, maybe enough to allow him to wear a *cornicello* necklace, his father said, "Not a drop, thank God," but wouldn't elaborate.

They headed to the edge of the Tenth Ward to pick up George. It was a neighborhood not familiar to Nils, beyond Wegman's grocery store. There were run-down houses, ugly concrete buildings, a laundromat with people milling around outside who turned to stare at them as they moved by. Nils wasn't even sure he'd be able to find his way home without Mark leading the way, and this made him uneasy, but he was also uneasy about meeting up with George. He was a little afraid of George, who was a year older and rough. George had supposedly spent time in juvenile hall, and it wasn't hard for Nils to imagine what kind of violent, lurid things went on there, especially at night. He was Mark's friend, but Nils had no idea how they knew each other. George was a head taller than Nils and Mark. He had a blunt face, vaguely pelagic; in fact, many years later, fishing with his second wife in the Gulf of Mexico, Nils hooked a big Jack Crevalle, and when it broke the surface, he thought of George for the first time in a long time.

But George was a reliable source of marijuana, and Nils and Mark wanted to save their cash for beer, so here they were. George lived on a block that was shortened by virtue of some kind of industrial shop at one end that smelled like burning rubber. The houses were close together, with small, patchy yards that slanted down sharply from the porches and crumbling steps that led to the sidewalk. It struck Nils that a father and son could not play catch in those yards. They climbed the steps and stood on the porch. Mark knocked on the screen door and called out. Nothing. Then they heard shouting, shoes scraping on a wooden floor, and what sounded like a slap. Mark looked at Nils and raised his eyebrows, and they both stepped back from the door. In a moment, it flew open, and George spilled out, muttering to himself. He didn't acknowledge them, just started toward the street, and they followed. He had a red handprint on his face, and to Nils it called to mind a painting in one of his father's American Indian art books, something put on the face before battle, or maybe to mourn, he couldn't remember. Mark jogged a little to catch up and walk beside George. "Jesus, he broke a lot of blood vessels with that one."

"Fuck it," George said. "I need a cigarette though."

Mark looked back at Nils, and Nils handed over a Marlboro. George had his own lighter, a fake Zippo with a green skull on the side. He lighted his cigarette and took a deep drag and exhaled the smoke through his nose. Nils handed another cigarette to Mark and took one for himself. George stopped abruptly, spun around, and stared at him. There was something of a threat in the air. "Who the fuck are you again?"

"Nils," he said. Then: "Mark's friend," regretting it right away because it sounded dumb and weak. George nodded and brought up his lighter. There was a breeze, and he cupped his hand around the flame, his fingers touching Nils's cheek, almost tenderly, until Nils had his cigarette lighted.

Nils was happy to see landmarks of his own neighborhood again. It wasn't a matter of clearly defined borders. It was more about what *felt* like his home turf, his knowledge of the intersections, of certain shortcuts, which stores were friendly, and which had people that would stop what they were doing to follow him and his friends around. They didn't particularly look like hoodlums, they didn't wear leather like those guys in *The Lords of Flatbush*, nothing like that, but their hair was long, and they may have looked like the kind of kids who were going to shoplift, which wasn't far off the mark. Nils himself was trying not to shoplift. His mother was a Lutheran minister's daughter, and when he began hanging out with what she called *marginal* kids, she began to worry. Doing the laundry, she found a gold lighter in his jeans pocket, a butane lighter that worked like a small torch. The fact of a cigarette lighter didn't seem to bother her as much as the idea that he might have stolen it. "We don't steal," she'd said, waving the lighter in front of his face. Her voice had been plaintive, almost desperate. "People in our family do not steal." He had assured her that no, he had not stolen the lighter; it wasn't even his, it belonged to Jamie Serio, someone he invented in the moment, she could call him and ask. They'd been using the lighter to melt plastic army men for a diorama on the Vietnam War, simulating napalm, and Nils happened to pocket it. The flood of specifics seemed to placate her. And in truth, he had not stolen the lighter. Mark had, from one of his mother's boyfriends, and traded it to Nils for a stash pipe Nils had bought at the head shop with money he had plucked from his father's wallet. It had struck Nils that everything could probably be traced to some kind of theft or another. Just how far back should one have to go, anyway?

At Norm's Liquors, they stood in the parking lot, away from the front window, and waited for just the right guy to come along. You had to be careful because the wrong guy could lead to trouble, the owner chasing you away, or even the police showing up. At the very least, some kind of morality lecture. You never asked a woman. And you never asked someone your father's age. This time of day, noon, there weren't many customers. George didn't seem to have much patience. Like some kind of animal in a cage, he paced around. Rummaged in the dumpster a bit. Pulled out an empty wine bottle and hurled it back, shattering it. Then a silver Grand Prix whipped in, playing Billy Joel very loud. A young blond guy climbed out, and Mark was on him, the designated spokesman because he was so smooth. Would the guy mind buying them a six-pack of Genesee? He could keep the change for his trouble. "Sure thing, little man," the guy said. His word was no guarantee; they'd had people come out and laugh at them and keep the money, tell them to fuck off. There were many outrages in the life of the underaged.

Nils looked over and saw George bent into the window of the guy's car. He emerged holding a pair of sunglasses, nice Ray-Bans with mirrored lenses. He dropped them into his shirt pocket. Nils was stunned; it seemed a great violation of some code. The blond guy was more friend than stranger. He glared at Mark, who shook his head quickly, *don't say anything, please.* Nils stepped back a few yards aiming for some physical metaphor. Lighted a Marlboro and feigned interest in the cloudless sky over the city. The guy emerged from the store with two bags, handed one to Mark. "The change is in there," he said. They thanked him, George the most profuse. They moved on, and Nils fought the urge to look back, to see if the guy was rummaging around for his sunglasses, not wanting to see the look of betrayal on his face when he realized what had happened.

They cut through the YMCA parking lot, threading between cars glittering and hot under the midday sun. Nils kept his eyes open for his father's car, the big red Matador station wagon. His father had started going to the YMCA, but Nils wasn't sure if it was over his lunch break or later in the day. They'd all been curious about what he did there. Did he lift weights? Was he taking judo? Did he swim? No, nothing that exciting, he only walked on the oval track. He had a small, zippered gym bag with nothing inside it but a pair of canvas low-top sneakers. They seemed awfully clunky for walking in but were no doubt better than the cowboy boots he'd worn as far back as they could remember. Nils had heard his parents arguing about the YMCA, or at least discussing it intensely, but he wasn't sure what the specific problem was.

They were bound for the Genesee River; this was the plan. Nils had never been to the river, though it was in the neighborhood, one of those landmarks that people tend to ignore when they live close by, maybe like New York City natives who never visit the Statue of Liberty. Nils and his friends were always in search of somewhere to hang out, away from prying eyes, trouble, people they didn't want to share their beer and marijuana with, the leeches who seemed to have a nose for where people were partying. There was a courtyard at a Catholic church where they liked to gather, and since Mark's mother worked during the day, they used his attic sometimes, by a window that carried their cigarette and marijuana smoke up and away. Mark had a portable record player up there, and a rug to sit on, and a Farrah poster to stare at. But it was very hot. Mark had recalled hiking down to the river when he was much younger, when his father still lived with them, how they had packed a lunch. Nils was immediately on board, he liked rivers; one of his favorite books was *Huckleberry Finn*, and after so many months in the city, he was looking forward to a little bit of nature, even if it meant having George along.

A steep dirt trail by the bridge led to the river. At a switchback halfway down, they met a young couple on the way up, hippie types. They seemed a little scared for a moment, and Nils realized it was George; he looked menacing without even trying. "Hey," the guy said. "We had a campfire down there, it's still burning."

"Thanks," Nils said, trying to counter George's sneer. "Appreciate it."

The couple nodded and hurried past, and Nils noted the guy's hand pressed against his girlfriend's back, silently hurrying her up the trail. He felt bad. He realized he was always on edge when George was present, waiting for something bad to happen, a fight, some spontaneous act of vandalism, like when George kicked in a taillight on a Pontiac they were walking by for no reason, making them have to run. Or what he'd done just a few minutes earlier, stealing the sunglasses. Mark was the opposite, and Mark was like Nils in many ways, cautious when it came to breaking the law, and purposeful. There was no reason to kick in a taillight if the owner didn't do anything to you.

At the bottom of the trail, the bank was sandy in between patches of trees and brush. Nils looked up; he could barely see the rim of the gorge, beyond which was Maplewood Park, there was too much vegetation. He could see the side of the bridge spanning the Genesee but not the cars going back and forth. He found it amazing that things were so natural in the midst of a big city. He felt stirred by it. It seemed like forever since he'd been anywhere remotely wild. In Iowa City, he had spent many hours in the ravine behind their house, following raccoon tracks in the mud by the creek, building a shelter with scrap lumber, whittling a bow and arrows with his pocketknife.

They walked down a ways and found the campfire within a ring of big stones. Nils sat on a log between the fire and the wall of the gorge. It was a tactical move. He loved being near the water, but one of his greatest fears was drowning; he had once slipped in a motel swimming pool and started sliding into the deep end. He could still remember that terrible panic, his frantic thrashing. If it had been just him and Mark, he would have sat anywhere, but he didn't trust George to not fuck around, try to push him into the river. Nils had tried to learn how to swim. He had an old Boy Scout manual from the 1950s, and he had studied the section on swimming, the diagrams of the various strokes, the instructions on how to tread water. The boys in the illustrations were always smiling, as comfortable in the water as they were on dry land. They made it look so easy, but when Nils tried swimming, he could not get his arms and legs to work together, and he always sank.

They opened beers, lighted a joint. It was cooler by the water than up above, and the heat from the fire felt good. A fire made hanging out that much better, Nils thought. There was something comforting about it that went back very far, to when people were trying to keep the cold and predators away. His book on wilderness survival recommended that you build a fire right away, the moment you realized you were lost, for psychological as well as practical reasons. Without a fire, you could quickly become dispirited, especially as night fell, the book said, and Nils thought becoming *dispirited* would be a terrible thing if you were alone in the wilderness, worse than being hungry.

George was telling a story about his aunt calling from the bathroom for her cigarettes. How he went in and found her in the tub, draped in bubbles. How she made him sit on the toilet to keep her company. "The bubbles kind of melted away, and I saw everything. First her tits and then everything else. Her black fucking *bush.*"

"That's crazy," Nils said. "That must have been something else."

George hacked up a loogie and spat it at the fire; it sizzled angrily like some defiant, living thing. "Haven't you never seen a naked girl?"

Nils admitted that no, he had not, at least not all at once like that.

George looked at Mark with the same question creased across his forehead. "A few," Mark said, and he wouldn't look at Nils.

George stood, stretched. He climbed around the base of the gorge, looking for more wood, kicking and tearing at limbs. He came back with a branch whose dirt-covered end was crawling with insects. Plunged that little ecosystem into the hot coals and laughed. He twisted the branch around and watched the flames slowly take hold. His cheek was turning dark red; the handprint had blurred into an amoeba-like bruise. Nils couldn't imagine. His own father never hit him or his brother or sister, despite them probably giving him reasons to. And Mark's father was one more weekend dad, afraid to do anything to alienate his kids. Their weekends together seemed to involve spending time at the mall, at restaurants, anywhere but his father's tiny apartment, which Mark had said reminded him of a motel room with a plastic coffee table and sailboat paintings on the walls.

The wood George had thrown onto the fire was mostly green and started generating a lot of thick white smoke. Nils had read enough Louis L'Amour novels to know you wanted to use dry wood to avoid calling attention to your fire. He looked up, trying to determine whether the smoke was dissipating before reaching the rim of the gorge or whether cars on the bridge would see the plume. The last thing they needed was the authorities showing up. They were breaking a bunch of laws, all at the same time. It was no wonder George had spent time in juvenile hall. He was careless, impulsive. Mark seemed to have the same concern about the smoke and walked sort of casually down the trail and came back with a dry log that looked like driftwood, nearly white, and poked around at the fire, moving the green branch to the side and raking at the coals before setting it down. The smoke thinned out. George didn't seem to notice or care.

Nils lighted a Marlboro. His head was thickening, and his mouth was dry from the marijuana. More and more, he liked being in this state, liked feeling both close to his thoughts and far away from them at the same time. This was good Columbian, and it was worth having to put up with George, he decided. He studied the river. You could hardly tell it was moving, the surface was so smooth. He looked around. Except for the fire pit, and the section of the bridge visible from their spot, there was no evidence of humans.

This wasn't the wilderness of British Columbia or the Amazon, but it was *something*. After his parents had announced they were relocating to Rochester, he'd gotten out the Rand McNally atlas and saw that big glaring yellow sprawl of city, so much larger than Iowa City. He had assumed there would be no place for him to be the outdoorsman he wanted to be. And he had been right in that assumption. He and his friends spent ninety-nine percent of their time on concrete or indoors. They drank, got high, and listened to albums, Rush and Kiss and Led Zeppelin. He thought those were things people should do *in between* doing more interesting things, but they didn't do the interesting things. Well, there were girls. Nils was going out with a girl named Sunda with big hair and fierce eyes, but *going out* didn't carry with it anything tangible. It was sort of symbolic. Her parents were strict and wouldn't let her roam around with the kids Nils roamed with, so he saw her mainly at school, passed her romantic notes now and then. He thought it was cute that she moved her lips when she read the notes. He had walked her home once and kissed her behind her father's plumbing van, which was pretty exciting. Now in the summer, they hardly saw each other and had to hope to be invited to the same birthday party, that kind of thing. She had four older sisters, so he could never get her on the phone, and when he did, she mostly complained about her sisters, and he could hardly get a word in edgewise, but he liked the sound of her hushed voice, liked knowing he was helping her by listening.

Something splashed in the water, but he looked too late to see what it was. He had no idea what kind of fish were in the Genesee. Catfish? Perch? He was a member of the Outdoor Life Book Club, and on his shelf was a heavy *Encyclopedia of Freshwater Fishing*, and he thought that might have the answers. There was no reason he couldn't do some fishing down here, he thought. He wasn't sure if Mark would be interested in fishing, but he might come along just to hang out. He imagined them bringing their girlfriends down there, Sunda and Mark's girlfriend Gina, Sunda's best friend; and by the way, Nils knew for a fact Mark had never seen Gina naked because she had complained to Sunda that when she was alone in her house with Mark, she wanted to make out, but he only wanted to brush her long hair, and she wanted to know if that was kind of weird. It was. Nils pictured himself standing on the bank with the Eagle Claw rod and reel he'd gotten for Christmas in Iowa and landing a good fish and how they'd be grossed out when he gutted and cleaned it but think it was delicious when he fried it over the fire, and Sunda would feel safe and provided for and lean against him while they watched the fire and drank some beer.

He glanced at George, and George was staring at him, and Nils took a drink of beer, trying to look nonchalant, and studied the label for a bit, and yes, George was still staring at him. His field of view narrowed, and the only thing in the universe was George looking at him and him trying to be cool, watching a drop of water work its way down the side of his beer can. He had wondered if George would get bored at some point and decide to pick on him. He flickered a glance at Mark, but he was leaning back with his eyes closed, head tilted, getting some sun. He hoped Mark would intervene if things got nasty, he seemed to know how to talk to George, and George seemed to respect Mark. Maybe Mark was his only friend. He was still looking at Nils through those round, kind of surprised-looking eyes, kind of expectantly, as if he were waiting for Nils to respond, to say, *what are you looking at*, which was always an invitation to fight, like saying *your mother* to any Italian kid, you could say that to an eight-year-old Italian kid and he'd throw a punch, it was guaranteed. Nils believed he was pretty tough, tough enough for seventh grade, anyway, for his own neighborhood, but George was like another species altogether. He was like a Cape Buffalo, the most dangerous animal in Africa. Nils had read an article on them in *Sports Afield*, how you had to shoot them in just the right spot if they were charging you, right in the brain, and their head would be moving up and down, and you'd be terrified and probably shaking. You could shoot them in the heart, and they'd keep coming.

It struck Nils that he could probably punch George in the face as hard as he could, and George wouldn't feel it. That bruise on his cheek did not seem to bother him. Nils took a sip of beer and held it in his mouth to dampen his tongue. Mark looked so relaxed over there, half asleep, not a care in the world. Well, Nils thought, if anything happened and Mark didn't back him up, he'd wait until he was alone with Mark, wait until much later, like in that Sicilian saying, *revenge is a dish best served cold*, and then kick his Italian ass and *good*. Really put a thumping on him. They'd fought before, the first time they met, on a January day right after Nils had moved to town. He had been standing in the front yard, watching wet snow come loose from roofs and slide down and drop silently to the ground. Two boys had come down the sidewalk, Mark and a kid named Gilzow. They'd stopped. Who was he, Mark had demanded. Nils had identified himself. Did he live here, they wanted to know, in this house? He did. Where did he come from? Iowa. "Oh, so you're a hillbilly," Mark said. Nils had seen nothing threatening in the conversation. In Iowa, he'd gone to a school largely populated by faculty kids, and fights were rare. So he had taken Mark's question at face value. *No*, he'd said, waving his arm horizontally. *Iowa is flat*. Mark had mocked him. "Iowa is flat," he'd repeated, with a southern drawl. Then Gilzow had chimed in. "Kick his ass, Mark," and Mark was upon him, punching him, a torrent of blows to his head and face, but within the surprise of it all, Nils had noticed that the punches didn't hurt, that they weren't any more consequential than his eight-year-old little brother's punches. Nils had punched back, kind of half-heartedly, still confused about the reason for the fight, and after a bit, Mark and Gilzow went on their way. "We aren't in Kansas anymore," was all his father had said, after Nils recounted the event. When Nils started school at Virgil I. Grissom the following week, he'd been a little nervous about the idea of running into Mark, but it was Mark who came up to him after their teacher introduced Nils, and said "Hey, it's Iowa man," slapped him on the back, and now they were best friends.

George stood up again. Nils braced for trouble, but George only found more branches and heaped them around the fire to create a sort of tipi-shaped structure. They were dry this time and caught fire quickly. "Check it out," he said, walking backwards a few feet. He ran toward the fire and leaped, legs out front, like a broad jumper. The pile of branches was high, and he didn't quite clear it, just crashed through the top of the fire. A long, curved, burning branch entered the raggedy cuff of his jeans. From his vantage point, Nils knew it a few seconds before George did. It seemed an impossible thing to happen. A confused look crossed George's face after he landed, and then he yelped, and it was that high-pitched yelp that would be the hardest thing to try to forget, a sound like an injured puppy, not the roar of a wounded bear. He slapped at his inner thigh and kept yelping. Then he lurched toward the river and dove in. Nils did not hear a splash. George just *entered* the water with the precision of an Olympic diver. Nils ran to the bank, and then Mark was there, too. They waited for George to surface. Nils headed downstream a few yards to a clear spot, but still nothing happened. "I can't help him," Mark said. "I can't swim."

"Me neither."

Things became very quiet. Nils could hear the water lapping at the edge of the bank. The fire crackled behind him. He kept thinking he saw movement in the corners of his eyes, but it was only the dappled sunlight on the water. He looked over at Mark, whose face was pale and frozen, in concentration or maybe something else. Nils returned to staring at the water. He couldn't think of anything else they could be doing. In his Boy Scout manual, drowning people were splashing around, you could see them having trouble. But George had just *vanished*. If they had a rope, one of them could safely get in the river and feel around for George. But they didn't have a rope. The nearest rope was probably a mile away. They might as well wish for a boat. He recalled the moment George realized his skin was burning, the shock on his face. How much time had passed before he was hopping stiff-legged to the river? Could he have tackled George like you were supposed to do with people on fire? Maybe he could have poured beer on his thigh. But it had all happened so fast, and his brain had lagged a few seconds behind, trying to catch up, and then George was gone, just like that. "Maybe he's fucking with us," Mark finally said. He pointed down the bank. "Maybe he knows how to swim underwater. He could be watching us right now, thinking this is funny."

"He could be," Nils said. "You know him better than I do."

They went back to the fire. Mark pried a beer from the six-pack ring and handed it over to Nils, then took one for himself. "I'll kick his ass if he's fucking with us."

"We'll throw him right back into the river."

"What was up with him, anyway?"

Nils realized that Mark was unaware of the burning branch in George's jeans. He pantomimed the event. "It went right the fuck *up there*, like, up to his balls, I think, and it was *glowing*. I mean, it was orange-hot."

"Jesus, no wonder he was screaming."

Nils nodded and sat down. He was acutely aware of the hard, dry ground under his feet, the endless supply of fresh air. He imagined George inhaling murky water, the air squeezing from his lungs, just a few yards away. How could it happen so quickly and quietly? Had he bashed his head on a submerged piece of concrete? The river looked so peaceful but who knew what kind of junk was right below the surface? Was he tangled in some debris, some twisted metal, some old chain-link fence? The surge of images was too much to bear. "Goddamn," he said, and took a long drink of beer. Lighted a cigarette and stared at the fire, now almost burned down to just coals.

"Should we be going for help or something?" Mark asked.

Nils couldn't imagine telling anyone about it. The fact of the beer and marijuana would come up. He pictured a cop listening to his story about the branch going up George's pant leg, how implausible that would sound, like something created to cover up a crime. His paranoia picked up steam, how would they explain the bruise on George's face when they found him, *you boys clubbed him, didn't you, and you drowned your buddy.* "No," he said. "Unless you want them blaming us for this."

"I was just thinking that," Mark said, because Mark was smart, he considered the implications, he had a strong survival instinct. They were both good at talking their way out of trouble. In the park once, a cop had spotted Mark's pot pipe sticking out of his pocket, the bowl, hooked in there like a pistol, and demanded he hand it over. Did the usual cop things, like studying it from every angle, sniffing it, all that. Mark had started crying and going on about his sister, how she had gotten into drugs and crime, ran away from home, went to treatment but relapsed, they didn't know what to do for her, their father was dean at the college, but all of his smarts didn't matter in this case, the pipe was hers and he wanted to get rid of it but was afraid someone else would use it, and just what was the best way to get rid of it, sir? Nils had nodded kind of gravely, enjoying this liberal lifting of the plot of *Go Ask Alice,* which they'd read in school, and the cop had ended up commending Mark, wishing him luck, and gave them each a coupon for a free ice cream cone at Baskin-Robbins.

Nils had no idea how long they sat there without George. The marijuana was doing its time tricks; it could have been ten minutes, could have been an hour, but after a while, without talking about leaving, they prepared to leave. Burned the plastic six-pack ring and the paper bag from the liquor store. George's second beer was unopened, and Nils held it in his hand, not sure what to do. Drinking it would imply acceptance of George's fate, and he wasn't ready to do that yet. It was too big an idea to work with. He placed it on the log George had been sitting on. It had the look of some kind of memorial. Mark reached down, picked up the Ray-Bans George had stolen. For a second, Nils saw their reflections in the lenses, and he was astonished at how young they looked, like two little boys. Mark flipped them into the river, exactly what Nils would have done.

They climbed the trail silently, like commandos. At the top, they were assaulted by motion and sound, cars rushing back and forth across the bridge. The smell of exhaust was overwhelming. Nils felt like he was going to topple over and had to grip the bridge rail for a moment. The light against windshields and concrete was harsh and unfriendly. It was like they'd been in another world, maybe another time, and had stepped through some portal, one that closed behind them. Forever. He knew they would never go back down to the river. There would be no fishing trip with their girlfriends. Sunda would never see him fighting a big fish. This was it, from now on, the city, with its broken warehouse windows and gritty air and people who always seemed anxious to fight.

They walked out on the bridge. Nils couldn't see where they'd been, the little beach, the fire. Below them, the Genesee was moving steadfastly up to Lake Ontario. He wondered if George would make it that far, if the river would shoot him into the lake, so vast and deep he would never be discovered. It would not, it turned out. George would be found a couple days later, snagged in some brush along the bank, not more than a mile from the bridge, not after any kind of search because nobody had bothered to report him missing, just an accidental discovery of an apparent accidental death, one paragraph in the *Democrat and Chronicle*.

Nils looked as far downstream as he could see. But it was all just shadows and glints of light. "Well," he said. "I guess he's fucked now."

"No," Mark said. He pushed away from the rail. "I'm pretty sure he was already fucked."

Nils had forgotten people were coming over. As he drew closer to home, he could see cars in the driveway and on the street. He was relieved. He could disappear, avoid being alone with his mother or father, the interrogation that might occur if they thought he looked troubled. He was glad they'd be drinking and socializing and less observant than they usually were.

Most of the people were in the living room. His father was in his chair, under a haze of pipe smoke, telling a story, holding up a photograph of the pet coyote he had when he was a young man in Arizona. Nils knew the story. It was the story of how a family friend came over and photographed the coyote in the garage, with dirt and snow spread on the floor and some bushes arranged to make it look like the outdoors, and how the friend entered the photograph in a national contest and won with his outstanding close-up of a coyote in the natural world. His father didn't acknowledge Nils. His mother was sitting at the dining room table showing one of the nuns how to crochet. There was a pile of beige yarn on the table, needles, ashes from his mother's cigarette where she missed the ashtray, bourbon in a jelly jar. "Sweetie," his mother said, glancing up at him. She sounded a little tipsy. "Say hello to Sister Celeste." Nils nodded, and the nun reached out and patted his arm. He met her eyes, and he wondered if his sin was on his face, if she was an expert at reading that, but she only smiled.

He went into the kitchen. Father Mulvaney was in there, preparing a lime for his gin and tonic. He had everything laid out neatly, the knife and tonic water and the Beefeater's, and he had brought down a clean plate to cut the lime on. Father Mulvaney was his father's boss, and evidently, they didn't always get along; they butted heads; his father said Mulvaney was too political and wary of taking on projects that could bring the wrong attention to the diocese. Or something like that. Nils didn't know any specifics, but he knew Mulvaney was the reason his father often came home in a bad mood and sat in his chair with a glass of Johnny Walker Red and listened to his Judy Collins record over and over again. Mulvaney always wore his black suit, his white collar. He was very tall, with peppery gray hair. He looked exactly like a priest or an airline pilot. Now he sort of grunted a hello. Nils opened the fridge but there was nothing good to drink inside. He filled a glass of tap water, drank it down. He was very thirsty. Filled another. Through the window over the sink, he saw his sister and two of her friends on the deck over the empty swimming pool. They were wearing shorts and tube tops, and he would have normally been interested in his sister's friends, they were voluptuous and sexy, but his mind was veiled by something dark and heavy. He was struck by jealously, that they could enjoy themselves without the terrible knowledge that someone had been swallowed up by the river that day.

He watched Father Mulvaney pick up one of the glasses his mother had set out for guests. He held it up to the light from the window, made a face, and rinsed it out before fixing his drink.

Nils realized he was probably never going to be alone with a priest like this, have this opportunity. He and his brother had started catechism classes but didn't get very far before dropping out. His father had not put up too much of a fight about it. He seemed to already be souring on the diocese, developing the same restless irritation they'd seen in Iowa right before they moved. "Can I ask you a question?" Nils said.

"Sure."

"What do you do," Nils said. His mouth went dry again. He sipped his water. "What do you do if you were there when something terrible happened, and it wasn't your fault, and you really couldn't do anything to stop it, but you feel like maybe there was more that you *should* have done, and you didn't tell anyone about it, either, when maybe you should have, because that could bring real problems?" He immediately felt like he sounded insane or stupid, like his classmates when they read run-on sentences aloud, an entire essay with no punctuation, the stuff that made their teacher, Mr. Price, press his palms against his face.

The priest pushed a chunk of lime onto the rim of his glass. "I would say, live *with* the guilt, not *in* the guilt."

Nils nodded. Father Mulvaney was looking out the window as if reflecting on the question, as if he were going to offer a little more guidance. If he had asked, Nils was ready to tell him the truth, the whole story, right there in the kitchen. He kind of wanted to. But then Father Mulvaney said, "How old is your sister now? Marie, is it?"

"Yes, Marie. She's sixteen."

"Ah," he said. "Well. She's filling out very nicely."

Nils sat on his bed with the *Encyclopedia of Freshwater Fishing* and paged through the species, looking at the color-coded habitat maps. There were probably salmon in the Genesee River, trout, bass, all kinds of fish, more than he would have imagined. Some of the same species appeared to also live in Lake Ontario. He wondered if the lake fish ever traveled upstream to hang out in the river, or if they remained in the lake, and if river fish resisted the current to stay in the river. It seemed to Nils they were dealing with two kinds of habitats. The lake fish could feel awfully cramped in the river and wouldn't be used to the steady push of the current. And the river fish might feel overwhelmed by all the space in the lake, might feel vulnerable. You'd probably be better off sticking with what you knew, he thought, with what you'd grown up with.

He pushed the book back in its place on the shelf and went to his window. Father Mulvaney was standing by the pool, looking up at the girls, drink in his hand. He was gesturing with his cigarette, and they were laughing. No, Nils thought, just because you could leave your natural environment anytime you wanted didn't mean it was a good idea.

In the Long Run

CHAMPION HELD UP A SQUARE of plaster wallboard. "We should save this, definitely."

Brita regarded her husband. He was standing atop a pile of junk in the trailer, wearing knee-high boots of the sort favored by British fox hunters—precisely the reason he had purchased them, mail order, from Orvis, she thought, or maybe L.L. Bean. This was back when Champion had been auditioning for a role in society as a sporting gentleman, a project that included the purchase of a three-thousand-dollar shotgun with gold engraving, the boots, a canvas coat featuring a game pocket, and an English Setter. Within a year, the dog had died, paying the ultimate price for her habit of chasing cars; the coat sleeves had paint all over them from when Champion wore it while freshening the white trim on their house; the shotgun was traded, unfired, for a Triumph motorcycle that consisted of dozens of parts in dusty wooden apple crates. Champion, who knew nothing of motorcycle mechanics, had gotten as far as polishing a few chrome pieces and soaking rusty bolts in gasoline before sweeping the parts to the corner of the garage in favor of restoring the crates themselves, which he was not half-bad at, and using them as curio shelves in his den. From the crates, he'd leaped to trying to restore a huge fire-damaged roll-top desk. This abandoned project was now in the trailer, along with broken radios, scraps of lumber, lengths of PVC pipe, a basketball backboard sans rim, half a doghouse, four feet of railroad track, and of course, Champion himself, who'd been trying to make room for an ancient water heater by jumping on the rest of the garbage before spotting the wallboard. "What do you think? Save it?"

"No," Brita said. She was attaching safety chains to the hitch on the pickup, trying to remember if she was supposed to cross them.

"What if we—what if I—get a hole in the wall and need to patch it? This would do the trick."

"Let's try not to make a hole in the wall."

"It happens," Champion said.

"Please, leave it in the trailer."

Champion stared at the white surface of the wallboard, squinting and moving it closer and farther away. Then he snapped it against his forehead. Very hard. It didn't break. He tried again and again until it shattered. "Ouch."

Brita laughed.

She was leaving him. She had told him; they'd discussed it at the dining room table which she had cleared of all distracting items, coffee cups and magazines, candles, anything he might be inclined to play with. They'd discussed it in the neutral environment of a booth at the Giant Panda Chinese buffet. They'd discussed it in the presence of their marriage counselor. Brita had made it clear this was a separation not of the trial variety. She had told Champion there was no other man, and in the main, this was the truth. She had not committed adultery. No lips other than Champion's had met hers in fifteen years; she could not fully remember what it was like to sleep with a man other than Champion; she could barely call forth the faces of boyfriends she'd had before he entered her life. So this was the truth but not the whole story. Because there *was* a man she was not so much interested in as she was open to *becoming* interested in. And knowing—well, *sensing*—that Bill Strandquist was interested in her had given Brita the last bit of courage she needed to leave. Bill Strandquist was a farmer from Hillsboro with a daughter attending

North Dakota State University. Strandquist was a patient in the clinic where Brita worked in registration. He had prostate cancer, but it was in pretty complete remission. He was a widower and drove a gleaming ten-year-old Ford F-150 pickup whose interior was pristine. Brita learned this when she went out to the parking lot to enjoy a little sunshine on her break and peered through the window and marveled at the dust-free dashboard, the absence of cigarette butts on the floor, the window itself squeaky clean. She had imagined the interior still smelled new. Bill Strandquist had come out and observed her through blue, merry eyes before asking if she liked what she saw. Brita, accustomed to having people come in and describe all manner of embarrassing afflictions, burning sensations, warts on testicles, had blushed. And she had mumbled something about wanting to buy a Ford pickup, and the next thing she knew, they were cruising down University Drive, her behind the wheel, and yes, it smelled new.

Champion insisted on driving to the dump. He claimed experience with trailers.

"When?"

"Before I met you. I had a travel trailer, and I went out to Montana. I went to Billings, Bozeman, Butte, Missoula, and then up to Glacier National Park. That's when I was big-time into photography. I had a Nikon F4 with a zoom lens. I wanted to shoot grizzly bears, but I didn't see any. I got some nice pictures of Lake McDonald, those smooth stones by the shore, kind of like abstract pictures. I mean, you can't tell they're stones right away. Not until you look real close. Kind of like those sand dune pictures that look like nudes. I wish you could see my photos. I'm pretty sure I left them at my brother's place. I could ask him to look around."

This was one of the problems with Champion. His mental tracks were laid like something from Six Flags.

They took gravel roads to the dump because Brita's father had suggested the old tires on the trailer he'd loaned them might blow out at highway speeds. "Then you'll be in high cotton," he'd said.

"High cotton. Isn't that a *good* thing?" Champion had asked, before Brita could glare him into shutting his mouth.

"What the hell do you know about it?" her father had asked. "Have you ever tried to find your way out of high cotton? You get lost in there forever."

"You're thinking of corn, I think."

"Corn, cotton, who cares?" Brita had said, pushing Champion out the door. Her father had coughed and growled from within. He was on oxygen for emphysema. "You know you're not supposed to upset him."

"People should know the truth," Champion said.

Champion often reminded Brita that they lived in an ancient lakebed. In particular, he liked to remind her of this when the sump pump failed and water spread across the basement floor. Everything essential was up on blocks, and you could see the stratification of water on the wood. The highest line was from the year they bought the house, ten miles from Fargo, across the Minnesota border. That was also the year that Champion began to get strange, well, *stranger*, moving from eccentric to something else. Maybe flat-out crazy, though she didn't think there was a name for what was going on with him.

"I like to imagine what it was like," he said now, "when all of this was under water. I mean, picture a huge prehistoric fish swimming right over there."

"Maybe you should slow down a bit," she said, looking at the wall of dust in the side mirror.

"Do you have any idea how long it will take to go twelve miles on gravel roads?"

"I'm just thinking about the tires."

He lighted a cigarette. "Twelve miles on gravel is a long twelve miles."

"We're not really in a hurry."

He slowed a bit. The road was soft, and the truck snaked from side to side, following the ruts. More than once, she grabbed the door handle, believing they were going into the ditch. They passed austere little ranches, places with three or four cattle, maybe a horse. Houses in apparently perennial renovation, with weathered plywood sheathing, half-shingled roofs. The land was changing abruptly from the platter of rich soil they lived on to a mangier sort of ground, and of course, Champion mentioned that a million years ago, they'd be in the process of emerging from the water. She nodded. When she'd first told Champion about the separation, she'd done it in front of their marriage counselor, and their counselor, wisely, had said, "You need to make this very clear, Brita. Are you intent on ending the marriage?"

"Yes, I am."

"Permanently?"

"Yes."

But even then, Champion had started rambling on about a couple he knew when he worked in California, how they were married and divorced twice before marrying yet again, this time for good as far as he knew. And this had somehow morphed into a discussion of United States Forest Service policy concerning forest fires and the logging industry, et cetera et cetera, until even their counselor simply gazed at Brita through tired eyes as if to say, *how have you managed for so long?*

Of course, she wasn't perfect either. She had, as they said, enabled him. Or at least she had long ago given up and allowed herself to fall into stasis. She sometimes viewed herself as a boulder half-buried in a pasture. By the time she tried to roll, the earth had been swallowing her for years.

"I've never been here before," Champion said. "On this particular road. I mean, we've lived around here for ages, and I've never been here. Isn't that something? We're only a little ways from home."

"That is something."

"It's a cool drive, don't you think?"

"Yes," she said. And it really was. They were so used to the grid-like farm roads of the valley that even a slight grade and occasional curve and band of gnarled trees made for quite a change. The windows were open and fresh air flowed across the cab, mingling with Champion's cigarette smoke. That was something she would not miss, the smoke. Bill Strandquist did not smoke. He had taken her for coffee, and while talking, she'd been astounded by his silence, how his attention had been on her, how she could not see him anxious to talk, impatiently waiting for the slightest gap, even a comma, like a fencer watching for an arm to drop before lunging in to take control of the match. Strandquist had shyly admitted that he didn't mind coming to the clinic because he liked to see her, that seeing her behind the registration desk made what followed a bit less arduous, and *arduous* was exactly the word he used.

"Maybe if we'd gone on more drives like this, you wouldn't be leaving."

"I don't think so."

A hawk swooped and flew parallel to the truck for a few yards. They both saw it, watched until it rose up and disappeared. There was, to Brita, something if not spiritual, then at least significant about seeing the hawk closely enough to discern the agate shine of its eye. *Please don't ruin this*, she thought.

And then she thought: *please ruin this.*

"You know why that hawk came near, don't you?"

"No."

"All the dust we're kicking up. He thought we were a tractor in a field. He was hoping we'd scare up a rabbit or a field mouse or something."

"Oh."

They missed the turnoff to the dump. Champion was positive they needed to go another mile, but after a mile, they were atop a hill from which it was plain to see no dump was in the area. They parked at an intersection. "We didn't really need to get rid of this stuff."

"We've been talking about it for years."

"You're leaving. Why do you care?"

"I don't know. I'd feel bad leaving you with all this crap to deal with."

Champion laughed one of his faux-hillbilly laughs. It grated on her like the washboard road. "That's rich," he said.

"You don't even say that."

"Say what?"

"*Rich.* That's not even something you ever say."

"Maybe I'm going to start."

She nodded. "That's your right."

"You're goddamned right it's my right. If I want to make the yard look like something from *Sanford and Son* that's my right, too."

"I know."

He spat out the window. "Well, I don't know where the hell we go from here."

One thing about Bill Strandquist was how he placed no demands on her whatsoever. He had not asked to call her. He had not laid a hand on her. The closest thing to intimacy he'd offered was opening the pickup door for her. Back at the clinic, before getting out of the truck, she'd said, "I'm getting a divorce."

And Bill Strandquist had just said, "Well, you've got to do that sometimes."

A pickup came up behind them, and when it slowly pulled around them, Champion leaned out the window and asked where the dump was. Brita used the opportunity to open Champion's glove box to see if a map happened to be inside. The glove box was wedged full of flattened cigarette packages, dozens of them, and they rained down to the floor. She tried to stuff them back in, but it was futile; the box would not latch. She let them fall to the floor again and kicked them underneath the seat and shut the box as Champion was finishing up his conversation. He watched the other pickup drive off. "What's so funny, you redneck?"

"What?"

"That guy. That camouflage cap illiterate bumpkin. He laughed at me."

"I'm sure he didn't laugh at you."

"He did. What's so funny about two people looking for the dump?"

"Did he say where it is?"

"Back a couple of miles. You know that big chain-link fence we passed?"

"The one I said might be the dump?"

"Yes." Champion cut the wheel hard to turn around in the intersection. His face was redder than usual. He stared straight ahead and picked up speed until they were going almost fifty on the loose gravel. She looked back and saw the trailer floating from side to side, like a kite's tail. She started to say something but bit her tongue. There would not be many more, if any, of these situations. She might or might not let Bill Strandquist take her out for coffee again or maybe even lunch. If things with him started to veer in any direction she didn't care for, she'd simply walk away.

"I mean, what's so funny about two people looking for the goddamn dump?"

"There it is," Brita said.

"Do you see a sign? You'd think there'd be a sign."

"No, I don't see a sign. Maybe it's on the other side."

"That's pretty dumb." Champion turned, and they found the entrance, paid for their load, drove around the little office building as the stench of garbage increased. And there it was, the dump. Across a canyon of trash, a huge Caterpillar with spiked iron wheels pushed garbage up a hill. Champion stopped the truck to watch. "Some of that is probably ours."

"I'm sure it could be."

"Look at all that garbage. No wonder it's so hard to find a dead body in a landfill."

"Jesus."

"It's true. They never find them. The cadaver dogs get all disoriented from the various aromas."

"Why do you think about stuff like that?"

"I watch the news."

She shook her head. Champion backed the trailer up to the residential dumping site. It took him several tries to get it done. She couldn't help but imagine that Bill Strandquist would have done it cleanly, in one shot, using the mirrors instead of climbing halfway out the window to see where he was going. It wasn't fair, she knew, and wasn't even appropriate. Her husband and Bill Strandquist were of two different worlds. Champion was a faculty child who had grown up in a house full of books. Champion's father had never taught him to use tools or play ball. Champion had studied Russian literature and came close to getting a doctorate before the dissertation hung him up. Now his income derived mainly from his trust fund and occasional translating gigs for refugee agencies in the area, usually at the courthouse. He left for those jobs in mirrored sunglasses and an olive drab flight jacket and acted as though he were a CIA agent. She doubted if Bill Strandquist had ever read Tolstoy or Dostoyevsky, but then again, knowing how to maneuver a trailer was probably more useful where they lived. Maybe even more useful in Russia.

They climbed out. The stench was even worse, if that was possible. She shielded her eyes against the sun and watched dozens of seagulls swirling around the Caterpillar as it worked. She wondered how the operator felt about the birds, if he was annoyed by them or viewed them as companions. Or if he no longer noticed them.

"Look at this," Champion said. He was pulling at a rectangle of cloth with a southwestern pattern of lightning and diamonds. Something yellow was smeared across the corner. "If I'm not mistaken, this is a bona fide Navajo rug." He came up to her. "Feel it."

"I don't want to feel it."

"Come on."

"It's garbage."

"People throw out good stuff all the time. Look at the pattern. See this?" He pointed. "See this white thread in the middle of all this blue?"

"Yes," she lied. She started undoing the bungee cords holding the tarp over their junk.

"I think it's the real deal. Did you know Navajos always weave an imperfection into their rugs?"

"No."

He wrapped the rug around his back and plucked a broken lamp from the trailer. "They do it because they believe that only the creator, you know, God or whatever, can make something perfect. They don't want to insult God by trying to make something perfect."

Brita climbed into the trailer and lifted the water heater over the rail. It landed with a dull thud on the soft ground.

"I bet I can get this paint off. Maybe I'll call the university. They might have someone in the art department who can tell me how to clean this. Of course, I might have to call the University of Arizona. Or New Mexico. Did you know the Navajo Reservation is so big it covers parts of three states?"

"That's interesting. Will you give me a hand with the grill?"

Together they wrestled the rusty old grill up and over. "We cooked a lot of burgers on that baby," Champion said.

Brita nodded.

Champion froze. He had spotted something else, evidently. His nostrils flared a bit.

"I thought we loaded that table with a hole in the middle," Brita said.

"I took it out," Champion said. "I'm going to cover it with thick linoleum, and it'll be good as new."

"Whatever," she said. She watched him kicking around while she continued to unload the trailer. This was the detritus, some of it, of twelve years in the house together. Hauling it away hadn't exactly been her idea. Their counselor had told her, while Champion was away getting a cup of coffee, that it would make sense to perform a few symbolic gestures to help him get the idea through his head that she was, in fact, leaving. They had agreed that it wasn't so much denial that Champion was dealing with but his own peculiar worldview in which everything worked out in what he always called "the long run."

She finished unloading and kicked scraps from the trailer bed. Champion wandered over, still wrapped in the rug, carrying a CD. "Pink Floyd," he said. "I wonder if it's any good."

"It's in the freaking *dump*."

"Maybe someone just got tired of listening to it." He rubbed it across his jeans. "It's hardly scratched. Do you want it? You have a CD player."

"No."

"I thought you liked Pink Floyd."

"Never ever did I like Pink Floyd."

He looked at her. His eyes revealed something that might have been clarity, might have been pain. She couldn't tell for sure. His lips quivered, and Brita thought he was going to speak, but he only shrugged and whipped the Pink Floyd. The CD sliced through the air toward the seagulls. Tilted and caught the sun and glittered like a jewel among the swirl of flapping wings, and for a moment, she thought, you couldn't tell it wasn't another bird up there, a different kind of bird, capable of staying aloft forever, but only if it really wanted to.

Mar Vista

LARSEN HAD BEEN OUT west for three months taking care of his father, mainly so that his father could die at home and not in a hospital away from his cats and briar pipe, and, at least in theory, in charge of his own life. Now his father was dead, and Larsen was finishing up a few details before heading back to North Dakota. The funeral home people had come to take the body to be cremated, and before they carried him downstairs, Larsen rested his palm on his father's head and was surprised that it was very warm, as if the gears in that powerful brain were still turning in death. The hospice people had then swept in and removed the bed and taken away the rest of his father's medications, lest they be abused, though Larsen had stashed several ampules of morphine in an empty milk carton in case he needed them later. His sisters were too bereft to be useful in the moment, keening in a way that sent the dog running to hide, though both had soldiered through the dying, especially with the intense horrors of bedpan duty.

Now they all stood in the living room, emptier than empty without their father's big mechanical bed and even bigger personality. Larsen felt untethered after so many weeks of purpose, entrenched routines, responses to crises like the clogged catheter and the small fire in the Pendleton blanket when his father's trembling hands shook coals loose from his pipe. Larsen knew this much: he had to get out of the house, right away.

His father had lived in Idaho, in a college town encircled by a wreath of low, cheerful, but uninspiring mountains. Larsen's father had chosen this place for retirement for reasons largely known only to himself. Even Larsen's mother, now five years gone herself, had been at a loss to explain the move, but as she had done her entire married life, moving from state to state every few years, she gamely went along. They lived up on a hill, in an area where the homes grew nicer the farther up you went, like some sort of living class metaphor. Not to say there were mansions at the top of the hill, but the yards and houses were bigger, and the people tended to have white-collar jobs. The Mormon bishop lived there. The neighborhood was too far up from the valley floor to make walking to stores or restaurants practical, and since Larsen had flown out, having been told the situation was dire, he had no wheels. He had thought he could use his father's Jeep but found it on four flat tires with some kind of rodent's nest clogging the air intake and a dead battery. His older sister didn't drive and relied on a Medicaid bus and taxicabs to get around after their father stopped driving, and his younger sister, like him, had traveled by air. Larsen had only been off the hill a few times, mostly with his three children who had made a pilgrimage at Thanksgiving to say farewell to their grandfather. They'd gone shopping and out to eat at Red Lobster, but it was hard for Larsen to enjoy, wondering what new crisis awaited him back at the house.

What he wanted most now was a haircut. His hair was shaggy from neglect, unmanageable, with a maddening tendency to veil his eyes. His daughter had said he was starting to look like a derelict. The social worker who came by every week had admonished Larsen to not neglect his own needs, but getting a haircut in the midst of tending to his father had seemed almost selfish. As a caregiver, he'd been like a commando behind enemy lines, focused solely on the mission at hand, unable to think of anything else, let alone dream of life beyond the war.

So this was job one, and when the cab arrived, he told the driver to take him to the nearest place where a guy could get a haircut with no appointment. "I'm not real picky," Larsen said. And so he was dropped off at a strip mall. It was a cold day, with bits of snow spitting from a gray sky, which only added to Larsen's gloom. But he attempted to be cheerful to the young woman who checked him in and led him through the salon to a chair in the back. He eased into the red vinyl and avoided looking at his reflection while the stylist snapped a black smock around his neck. She stood behind him and played with his hair.

"What do you have in mind today?"

He had nothing in mind. He was no longer married, not involved with anyone, so he had nobody's wishes to consider. He recalled when his wife had come home with her lovely long auburn hair chopped away, leaving behind a spiky hairdo that made her look like Kris Jenner. When he objected, albeit too late, she'd flown into a rage about control over her body, and this rage seemed to last until they were divorced a year later. "Listen," he said. "I'm way overdue for a haircut. I really don't care. I'm in your hands."

"Cool," she said. She was a waifish girl with a green and red mushroom tattooed on her thin bicep. Any other time he might have asked her about it, but he didn't have it in him and hoped that his silence would prompt the same from her. It didn't. While she snipped and combed, she asked what he was up to today. And what could he say? That a few hours earlier he'd checked on his father only to watch black bile spilling over his dry lips? How he'd plugged in the suction machine to clear his father's airway, but he was already dead?

"This is it," he said. "This haircut. It's my only plan."

She laughed and got to work. She told him about her pet rabbit, how it had disappeared in her apartment, how she'd looked under the bed, in closets, calling out for it the entire time. A mystery. "I was panicking big time. Like, how does a rabbit just *disappear*?"

"Did you look in a top hat?"

She didn't get the joke. "Well, he was behind the fridge. He was *stuck*. He's a roly-poly but he got back there somehow. Now I jammed a pillow in there to keep him out."

"Good plan," Larsen said.

The rabbit was litter-trained, she told him. He could do tricks, balance a treat on his nose. "My children had rabbits when they were little," Larsen said. "But they didn't do any tricks." He couldn't remember much about them, even their names, but he recalled how swiftly they tended to die, hopping across the lawn in one moment and then kicking spastically for a few seconds and expiring. It was disturbing to the children, and the only remedy was to quickly get a new rabbit to replace the lost one.

She turned on her clipper, edged his sideburns and the back of his neck, took care of some wiry renegade eyebrow hairs, cleaned up his ears. "What do you think?"

"Perfect," he said.

"Can I ask you something?"

"Sure."

"Are you an avid fisherman?"

It was a real non sequitur and took him aback. His first thought was that he bore some aroma from his father's house, which was a pantry of aromas, most of them unpleasant: cat urine, the bedpan, stale smoke, the various medicinal creams. But no fish odors that he could remember.

"I ask," she said, "because you seem like someone who would be an avid fisherman."

Larsen only nodded. He didn't have the energy to ask what had led her to this conclusion. He didn't consider himself an avid fisherman, but he didn't mind being mistaken for one. It was better than being mistaken for an accountant or gym teacher. Then he recalled that he in fact had been *thinking* about fishing a few days earlier, after finding his father's ancient but razor-sharp Finnish filet knife in the back of a desk drawer, a knife he had not seen nor thought of since he was a child. They were living in Iowa City at the time. Larsen was a nine-year-old with a keen interest in hunting and fishing, poring over copies of *Field and Stream* and *Outdoor Life* he snuck into the grocery cart when his mother was distracted. His father had been quite a sportsman in his own youth and liked to regale his children with tales of deer hunting, catching a record perch in Kansas, serving as president of his high school rifle team, but was too busy with work, or too lost in his own thoughts, to introduce Larsen to these endeavors. There had been many unkept promises of impending excursions. Finally, not really knowing what he was doing, Larsen got hold of some hooks and line, a can of sweet corn, and went down to the creek that trickled along the railroad tracks just beyond Roosevelt School. He'd found a stick to use as a rod and dropped a hook baited with the corn into a deeper pool where the creek entered a pipe, and miracle of miracles, a fat fish was on the line. He had been too excited to continue fishing and rushed home with his trophy still flopping. His father had pronounced it a bluegill and then went to his room, returned with the knife, and showed Larsen how to scale the fish with the back of the blade before taking off the fish's head, gutting it, and cutting it into two small chunks. Larsen had never seen the old man cook anything, even a can of soup, but he heated butter in a pan, laid the pieces inside, seasoned them with salt and pepper. Then placed each piece on a plate and they sat at the table to eat. His father had asked for the story of the fish. Larsen didn't have enough experience to embellish, but his father listened to the straightforward if not lackluster account, nodding sort of gravely, before returning to his chair in the living room, laying his worn briefcase across his legs, and going back to work. It was the closest they'd ever come to going fishing together. Larsen had not thought about that in years, not until he gripped the wooden hilt of the knife, as if the memory had been trapped in there for decades.

There was a problem with Larsen's direct flight from Salt Lake City to Fargo, for which, on short notice, he had paid handsomely. Fargo was locked in a late winter blizzard that was expected to last at least a couple of days, and the airport was closed. One of the televisions on the wall was tuned to the Weather Channel, and much of eastern North Dakota appeared as a huge, bright orange, Oriental Poppy. Larsen felt less dismay than simple resignation. Of course there was a blizzard. Why not, on top of everything else? The gate agent asked if he'd been skiing. "No," he said. "I've been watching my father die for three months, and I just want to get home."

"Hang on," she said. She tapped away at her terminal, then made a phone call, turning slightly away as she spoke. She glanced back at him a few moments later. "He seems okay," she said into the phone. He was trying to imagine what he might do in Utah for a day or two. He was three hours by shuttle from his father's house, and even if he were closer, he couldn't bear to walk back in after the protracted goodbyes to his sisters, his nephews and nieces, his brother who was supposed to handle the financial mess left behind. Larsen knew nothing of Salt Lake City. The Mormon Tabernacle Choir. Was that still a thing?

The ticket agent hung up and smiled broadly at him. "There's a plane leaving for Minneapolis in half an hour. That gets you closer, and there are a bunch of flights to Fargo every day from there, so you can probably go standby on one of them as soon as the storm passes."

"Well," he said. "I do appreciate it."

There was something unusual about the flight. Larsen seemed to be the only one on the dimly lit plane. The agent had led him personally to a gate and sent him down the chute. With no direction, he settled into a seat in the rear of the plane to await further instructions. Now he started to panic a little, wondering if he had been forgotten about, like those small children they find sleeping on a school bus having missed their stop. If it could happen to a child, it could happen to him, couldn't it?

Through the window he watched a utility vehicle pull up and a bulky figure start spraying a great mist of de-icer over the plane. It was about the last thing Larsen wanted to see. The process seemed an awfully simple one for having such a vital role in keeping the plane aloft. He wasn't really a timid flyer, but his father was dead, and you heard stories about someone dying and then a family member dying in a terrible accident the same day, that kind of thing. *Mr. Larsen was on his way home after his father died when the plane went down.* The sort of irony a local journalist would love to work with. He began to think his survival depended on leaving the plane, but then the engines began to whine, and they were moving away from the gate.

A flight attendant came down the aisle, and a little mystery was solved. This wasn't a regular flight, it was some sort of deadhead, whatever that was, and who did Larsen *know* to accommodate him like this? An entire plane, all to himself. "Are you some kind of VIP?" she asked, but jokingly. She sat down beside him and patted his knee. "I'm sorry to hear about your father."

Larsen was a little stunned. "Excuse me?"

"Ginger told me. You know, Ginger. At the gate."

"Ah," Larsen said. "Thanks. It's a tough thing. He was a good man."

They were taking off. No safety lecture, no worries about seat belts. He thought this must be what it was like to own a jet and wished he were in a better frame of mind to enjoy it. "I'm London, by the way." She offered her hand, and he took it, and that warmth, that human contact from a pretty young woman with impeccable makeup and a thick blond braid was almost more than he could bear. He did not want to let go. "And yes," she said, "I know London sounds like a stripper's name, but I was *conceived* in London, my parents were there for a Pink Floyd concert. If I was a boy, they were going to name me Gilmour after David Gilmour. Or David. They couldn't decide."

"I like it," Larsen said. "I think it's great when a name has a story behind it."

She stared at him. "Do you want a drink? We aren't really stocked, but I bet I can scare something up."

"Yes." What did he want? "Surprise me," he said.

He looked out the window. He imagined they were over the Great Plains by now. He saw no smear of light, no cities. Larsen thought about how in a matter of two minutes they'd go farther than a wagon on the Oregon Trail went on a good day. Larsen was a bit of a history buff, something his father passed down to him. The old man had been a professor of American Indian studies, part of the anthropology department, though he detested many anthropologists for what they did to the Indians. His father liked that Floyd Westerman song "Here Come the Anthros," *and not a cent of funded money that the anthros get to spend is ever given to their disappearing feathered friends*, and in his father's last days, Larsen had played him that one, yes, from the album *Custer Died for Your Sins*, and a lot of his favorite music, Marty Robbins' "El Paso," Woody Guthrie, anything he could remember his father liking, especially if it was rousing. By then his father was in a strange place, not completely unconscious but not responsive, either. But when Larsen played Willie Dunn's song about Louis Riel, his father raised his fist, so something was getting through the fog.

London came back with plastic cups and a can of Seven-Up and a handful of Seagram's miniature bottles. She handed the cups to Larsen and divided the Seven-Up, squinting at the levels, and poured a bottle into each cup. Then waggled her eyebrows and poured another bottle into each. "We don't have any more Seven-Up, so we have to maximize this drink."

"I'm on board with that," Larsen said. "Seven and Seven is my favorite drink, by the way."

"I know," she said. She looked around conspiratorially. "We know everything, Mr. Larsen."

"I'm beginning to think that."

"Well, thank the soda gods. We had a Seven-Up, and what else are you going to put in there? Not tequila."

Larsen raised his glass. "It's perfect."

She raised hers. "To empty planes."

"Yes." He took a sip and felt it burn all the way down. He was happy to feel something, even if just a physical sensation. His time with his father had been so consumed with action he had not really had time to feel much. If anything, he'd felt what he was ashamed of feeling, mainly irritation. His father had kept a rusty cow bell tied to his bed rail for emergencies and took to clanging it in the middle of the night to call for Larsen, who would rush up the stairs imagining the worst only to find out the old man had forgotten what he wanted, or thought, at three in the morning, that it was much later and time for everyone to get up. This happened more and more often toward the end, and Larsen lost his patience a few times. He had gone weeks without getting a full night's sleep. He confided in the hospice nurse who told him this annoyance was absolutely common among caregivers and suggested he talk to the social worker. He had not.

It was hard not to notice how London's skirt rode up past her knees, that stretch of shiny black nylon running from the top of her leather boot to the bunched-up hem, as inviting as any moonlit river, the Seine, glittering snugly against Paris, even the Mississippi dappled in refinery lights down south. Only a little booze, he thought, and here comes the lust and poetry. London was easily young enough to be his daughter.

As if to punctuate this line of thought, the plane banked very hard to the right and dropped rather suddenly. Larsen's stomach rose, and he was pinned to the window by gravity, and by London, before the plane leveled out. London made no move to separate herself from him. She'd gone from the aisle to the middle seat. She held up her drink. "Didn't spill a drop."

"We're no amateurs," Larsen said, holding up his own. He thought about asking why the plane had done that, but really, what better barometer for gauging the seriousness of a problem than a flight attendant, and she seemed unfazed.

"You know you could sit up in First Class if you wanted."

"I'd feel guilty, like I was getting away with something."

She laughed. "I get it. Anyway, all the cool kids sat in the back of the school bus when I was growing up."

They went silent for a bit. He was afraid she'd leave if he didn't say anything, but he could not think of anything to say. He felt so blunt from his time in Idaho. He wondered if he would be able to get back to work on his novel, if he could regain the momentum his trip had interrupted.

"Well," she said. "*My* father wanted me to be a pilot."

"Really?"

"See, he always wanted me to be *more*. More, more. When I played basketball, he wanted me to be point guard, right? And he thought I should *pitch* in softball and not play right field. That kind of thing. So why a flight attendant when I could apply myself and fly the plane? It took me a long time to realize he wasn't disappointed in me, he just believed in me *too much*, right? Do you understand? He meant well, it just didn't always feel that way. Anyway, he's fine with me being a flight attendant, now that he sees I love my job. How about you?"

Larsen wasn't sure if she was speaking to him as a father or as a son. He saw something of himself in her description of her father, though. But he hadn't mentioned having any children. "My father, and my mother, they expected us kids to find something to be passionate about and do that thing the best we could." It was true, but there were caveats. His parents disapproved of working only for money. They believed one ought to do something meaningful, though they were flexible in what *meaningful* was. It seemed to involve various forms of selflessness and sacrifice.

"Was your father proud of you?"

Larsen took a sip of his drink. It was warm now, like something teenagers would sneak into a school dance. But still good. "I guess he was," Larsen said.

"Well, did he ever *say* so?"

He tried to recall and couldn't. There seemed to be an implicit pride. Larsen had noted upon arriving in Idaho that his father's top bookshelf in the living room was displaying Larsen's two novels and his story collection and the literary journals he had faithfully mailed his parents over the years. He could not recall seeing them like that on earlier visits, so he'd been unable to escape the niggling idea that the shelf arrangement was fresh, meant for Larsen to notice, a subtle manipulation to keep him from leaving. He had no idea whether his father had even read his work and never asked. His first novel was dedicated to his parents, and they never mentioned the dedication, so who really knew? His father did prefer literature that spoke to some higher truth, that might enlighten a reader, spur them toward action in a worthy cause. He had made Larsen read *The Grapes of Wrath* when he was eleven. Larsen's own work was, he liked to believe, concerned with something more universal, Faulkner's idea of the human heart in conflict with itself, though he wasn't sure he even understood what that meant. Perhaps he had it all wrong and was simply trying to justify his stories, which seemed to involve people too consumed with their own problems to worry about the greater good. Perhaps his reluctance to discuss his work with his parents came from the same place as not telling them when he and his wife had taken a Caribbean cruise, that unless they'd been thatching roofs in Jamaica, instead of floating drunkenly down the White River in Ocho Rios on inner tubes, the entire trip would be seen as frivolous. "I'm sure he did tell me," Larsen said.

She kissed him, then. She was either aiming for his lips and missed, or aiming for his cheek where it met the corner of his mouth and hit it dead on. He hated this kind of ambiguity, it was like someone shouting a question in a loud bar, you had to guess, and you could easily say the wrong thing in response. It struck him that much of his life had been spent responding and reacting improperly to ambiguity. The higher the stakes, the worse he performed. London gulped down her drink. "Chug that," she said, and he did. She tossed the plastic cups over the seat and moved in again and excised the doubt. There was some necking, soft and sweet. He ran his hand under her skirt and up her thigh, more out of habit than some great organic drive. But she pushed his hand away and said, "My grandmother says that regret lives below the waist."

"She's not wrong," Larsen said. They resumed this PG-rated film. He marveled at how smooth and firm her cheeks were. She kept her eyes open. She allowed him a little fondling through her blouse. He thought he could live this way forever, imagining a plane that stayed up indefinitely, catching the right air currents like a vulture. That would be okay, he thought. But the plane swayed again and dipped, and he felt his insides lift. He heard the landing gear deploy, those alarming *thunks*. London cocked her head. "It's gonna be a rough one," she said. "Crosswinds. We'll be going in almost sideways. Are you up for that?"

"I guess I have to be." But he felt his heart beating faster, his palms start to dampen.

She laughed, locked her mouth over his, and took control of his breath until it was all over.

The blizzard had lost intensity, and the Fargo airport would be opening up, but there wasn't going to be an available flight until tomorrow. Larsen was at that point in a journey where people desperately just want to get *home*. He'd actually hit that point soon after getting to his father's house, after realizing it wasn't going to be the short stay he'd imagined when his father called and, in a wheezy, old-man's voice, asked him to come out right away. Larsen had assumed this was a deathbed request and left the next morning, leaving certain matters postponed, bills on the table, perishables on the counter. He'd packed only a few things in a backpack and, on the flight to Salt Lake City and subsequent shuttle into Idaho, worried that his father was succumbing with every passing mile marker. He had talked to his older sister, but she was a chronic hysteric and kept repeating, *we need you, we need you.* Then Larsen had walked through the door to find his father looking remarkably hale and hearty, watching *Shane*, his favorite movie, the only sign of infirmity a catheter bag laying casually on the carpet between his feet. His wheeze absent.

Larsen wasn't cynical enough to think he'd been hoodwinked, but it wasn't a stretch to imagine his father exaggerating a bit to speed things up. He had been a great strategist during the civil rights movement in Mississippi in the early 1960s, organizing successful boycotts, non-violent marches, lunch counter sit-ins. He'd been mercilessly clubbed by angry police but saw even this as a way to engender support and sympathy for the cause, especially when this act was photographed and distributed over the wires to newspapers all around the world. When Larsen was washing his father's jaundiced head, he saw the stringy scars from those hickory nightsticks, like ancient riverbeds viewed from space. So his father was shrewd enough to hasten his arrival by implying the end was at hand. His doctor made house calls, and after one visit, Larsen followed him outside and asked point blank if his father was really dying. His kidneys were failing, Dr. Burley said, and there were associated heart issues and a great risk of infection, but everything went back to the kidneys, people needed to understand that, did Larsen understand that? Yes he did, but were we talking a matter of a year? Months? Weeks? Dr. Burley offered a long medico-politico answer that cleared up nothing but then sort of cryptically suggested that Larsen make Thanksgiving as celebratory as possible with as much family as he could muster. But it was clear enough to Larsen, then, that he could not go home, that he was in it for the duration.

He had a cousin in Minneapolis. Frank, from his father's side, was an artist who made extremely large versions of iconic American toys but with some kind of ironic twist. A six-foot fiberglass GI Joe in a tight red dress; a life-sized Barbie Corvette, upside-down and accordioned against a tree, with Barbie spilling from the wreckage. Pretty nifty stuff, and Larsen had even driven his children down to see an exhibit when they were younger. But the work was impractical for home display, and although Frank had sold a few pieces to youthful companies, software startups, that kind of thing, most of his stuff was jammed into a storage unit. He had once said he envied Larsen because Larsen's work was the size of a book.

He had not seen Frank in several years, but Frank, on the phone, betrayed no great shock at hearing from Larsen. "Your father," he said. "I opened the paper and I'm like, what the fuck, there's my uncle in the obituaries. I couldn't believe it. I had to read about it in the newspaper like everyone else."

"Everything happened so fast," Larsen said. "We haven't had time for proper notifications." That much was true. The day after his father died, the phone started ringing, with journalists calling from across the nation. That iconic photograph of his father on one knee in the street, getting beaten by three grimacing policemen, was still out there decades later, showing up in history books or as still shots in documentary films. Larsen's children were ecstatic to see the photo in their middle-school social studies textbook, with the caption serving as proof to their teachers and peers that it was, indeed, their grandfather. They'd never gotten a chance to know the old man very well, but this mythologized version of him was probably worth any number of Easter dinners.

Larsen and his brother had divided up the task of speaking to reporters from New York, public radio, Mississippi, the local news, and almost every city he'd lived in over the years. But first they'd sat down to draw up three pages of notes covering everything, from his father's complicated timeline to his favorite quotation, that IWW motto, *an injury to one is an injury to all*, not wanting to leave anything out, or worse, to provide differing accounts. Their father was a stickler for accuracy, and they'd felt his presence looking over their shoulders, *don't forget this, don't forget that*. The interviews were sort of grueling, and there were plenty of dumb questions, and the reporters seemed uninterested in everything his father had done before and after that three-year stint in Mississippi, though Larsen's brother, himself a journalist, had pointed out that in Neil Armstrong's obituary, nobody cared what happened after he returned from the moon. In any event, they were so busy with this, nobody did much in the way of calling friends and family, though it never would have occurred to Larsen to notify Frank anyway. They weren't close.

"Well," Frank said. "I'm sorry as hell."

Larsen explained the situation. He was trying to get home, a flight was unlikely even in the morning, the roads were questionable, but would Frank be willing to drive him three hours to Fargo? He could promise a nice meal and gas money, of course. It was asking a lot, he admitted, at night and on short notice. "I'm just worn out," he said.

"I'll be right there," Frank said.

That was a relative phrase in the big city, but it wasn't very long before Larsen's phone chimed, and Frank announced his arrival. Larsen stepped into the cold night. Three months in a more temperate climate, with Idaho sort of in the outer thrall of the warm Pacific, had weakened his resistance to subzero temperatures. He had no substantial winter wear. He scanned the line of cars. When he had last seen Frank, his cousin had owned a big four-wheel drive pickup, fit for carting his creations around. But he couldn't remember more than that. He headed toward the only pickup in sight, but heard his name called and turned to see Frank halfway out of a tiny Mini Cooper with a Union Jack painted on the roof. It seemed a bizarre match, this compact car and Frank, who was a lean six-foot-five. Larsen felt a little like he was betraying his father by even getting into the car; his father had despised the English for what King George did to his Abenaki ancestors, putting a bounty on the heads of babies. And too, the old man considered himself something of an Irish Catholic, though his ancestry was thin and his relationship with the church was tumultuous.

Larsen accepted Frank's attempt at a hug across the bucket seats. How was the flight? Inconsequential, Larsen said. He thought of London, the taste of her breath, a little boozy and sweet, that embrace as they slipped through the clouds. It was a story to hold in reserve, for the right audience, the right moment, and this wasn't it. A flight for the ages, though now, like in that Pink Floyd song, he was just an *earthbound misfit* again. But the car was warm, and an overflowing ashtray gave Larsen the answer he was hoping for to the question of smoking. He had not had a cigarette since walking into the Salt Lake City airport. He lighted one and took a long drag. "What happened to your pickup?"

"Didn't need it anymore."

"What about your big, what would you call them, *sculptures?*"

"I don't do them anymore." Frank went quiet to focus on passing, darting ahead, changing lanes, shifting gears. He was one of those people who put their entire body into the act of driving. Larsen was relieved that the interstate was largely dry and clear, but he also knew that they were heading north and west, and things could turn on a dime.

"You're done with the big toys?"

Frank found a speed he felt comfortable with and leaned back. "You can thank your Dad for that, actually."

"How so?"

"He was on my mailing list, you know, for gallery shows and whatnot. You should be, too."

"I am," Larsen said, though he could not recall getting anything recently.

"Well, your Dad, I'll call him Uncle Jack, that's what I always called him. Uncle Jack sent me a note. Congratulations, all that. But here's the thing. He said that it seemed to him that I had satisfied an artistic vision and that I should try to grow from there, you know, move *forward.*"

"That sounds like Dad," Larsen said. "He hated stagnation. He was always looking for new dragons to fight."

"Yes," Frank shouted. "That's exactly how he put it. Look for new dragons to fight."

"It makes sense," Larsen said, and it did, and it was how he always explained all the moving around the family had done, following his father from job to job, to Iowa and Chicago and upstate New York, North Dakota. But there was a cost to that kind of vagabond life, and it was often the family that paid the price. They had never owned a stick of new furniture or allowed themselves to dream of attending any but nearby state colleges. Larsen was reminded of what Hemingway had said, that in the home of a starving artist, the artist at least had his art to sustain him, while everyone else was simply starving.

"I was hurt at first, to be truthful. It *stung*. But then I was finishing up what would be my last large-scale toy piece, a bunch of those Fisher-Price people, remember, they were cylindrical, made of wood, at least at first, before they went to plastic like everything else."

"Yes," Larsen said. "We had those, growing up. There was an airport, and little cars. You had to add some imagination when you played with them."

"Yeah. Well, I was looking at them and I thought, just what the *fuck* are you doing here, Frank? Are you even trying to say *anything*?"

Larsen nodded. "I think the whole approach was pretty cool, though."

"It was if I just did a few. Really, I should have just done that big GI Joe. I don't know. But Uncle Jack was right. I was being totally repetitive. So I shitcanned everything. Now I'm doing some mosaics out of broken toilets and sinks I get from house renovations. The first thing they always do is tear out the bathrooms."

"I like it," Larsen said.

"Uncle Jack never said that kind of thing to you?"

"No."

"That surprises me."

Larsen nodded, lighted another cigarette. He had a lot to make up for. "Why does that surprise you?"

"Well, I mean, I've read your stuff, and I love it, man, but *you* get kind of repetitive as well."

"How so?"

"You know. Your characters get into some kind of trouble, some kind of predicament, and then deal with the consequences, and then have some kind of epiphany but usually too late to do anyone any good. I'm not saying it's bad, but you do have a pattern."

Larsen started to object but bit his tongue. Reviewed his body of work in his mind. Frank was right, but couldn't that classic narrative arc be found in almost every writer's work? Tolstoy, De Maupassant, Flannery O'Connor, Carver? Of course, there were the Barthelmes, the Barths. Borges. But that experimental stuff always seemed more like improvisational jazz. Did anyone really connect to it emotionally the way they connected to a regular story, to Annie Proulx's *Brokeback Mountain*, for example, which Larsen had just re-read because his father had saved the *New Yorker* it appeared in for over twenty years in a Papago basket beside his chair? Life was stories, Larsen always told his students whenever he had a teaching gig. "I guess I never really thought much about it," he told Frank. "I do it the only way I know how to."

"Man, I get it. I do."

Larsen felt some irritation bubbling up. "And I'm limited, you know, to twenty-six letters. I can't smash up a toilet when I've used them up."

Frank laughed. "There's that Larsen sarcasm. I was wondering when it would show up."

"Sorry," Larsen said. "Really, I'm just totally fucked up from three months out there. You know it wasn't exactly like walking into the Brady Bunch house."

"Do they still have all those cats? That's what I'll always remember about you guys. That cat scene, you know? Cats walking around on the kitchen table. Licking the butter and nobody cared."

"It's less of a scene now."

"I like the memory, though," Frank said.

Closer to home, the road had swirled with blowing snow, creating that vertiginous effect that can send novice drivers over the shoulder and into the ditch. But underneath, the surface was largely unaffected. This had been primarily a ground blizzard, a wind event, without the heavy snow clean-up in its aftermath to further demoralize everyone. Now, back in Fargo, Frank passed on Larsen's dinner invitation, his suggestion that Frank spend the night and head back in the morning. His cousin had been hit with inspiration, talking about Larsen's father, and wanted to get back to Minneapolis and start on a new piece honoring his uncle. "A tribute."

"He'd like that," Larsen said.

Larsen brewed coffee for Frank's travel mug. He'd left for Idaho without throwing away the filter in the coffee maker and discovered a mound of moldy grounds waiting for him. He was at first relieved that Frank was not staying--his cousin had an energy that was taxing--but as he said goodbye and watched Frank hurrying out to his strange little car, he felt a wave of loneliness. He had not really been alone for months. His father's house had been a beehive, between his sisters, the visits from relatives, the hospice nurses, Dr. Burley, the cheerful kid who brought over liquid morphine and Ativan lotion every few days, and the nice Mormon neighbors with their casseroles, the same neighbors who had complained about the unruly Russian olive tree whose branches swept over the sidewalk and the sweat lodge in the back yard, from which they might see his father emerging naked now and then before he was housebound.

He called his sister to let her know he was home. She had not stopped crying yet and could not be consoled. Except for a brief, failed marriage, she had never left home. He called his children to let them know he was back. They promised to come by the next day. The death must have seemed like an abstraction to them, Larsen thought. They loved their grandfather but were young enough, in their early twenties, to see anyone over thirty as old. An eighty-five-year-old man must have seemed like some dry, brittle fossil that was hard to imagine had ever been a real living thing.

He walked around his quiet, stale-smelling house like it was some museum exhibition of his life before his father died. Apples in a bowl had turned brown and caved in. The manuscript pages on his desk were dusty. He picked one up and scanned it. His protagonist was on the top of a parking garage spying on his wife across town with a powerful celestial telescope. Larsen read a little more, hoping this was an unintentional metaphor, but it wasn't. He set the page down. Was he different than he was before abruptly heading west? Was he more philosophical, more aware of his own mortality? He didn't think so. Sadder? He wanted to be. He was still waiting for the emotions to hit, for the tears to come. His brother, always a tough guy, had been a mess of snotty-nosed sobbing, especially when the plain cardboard box of ashes arrived by courier, before numbing himself with Jack Daniels and Diet Coke. Everybody in the family, except his older sister, drank alcohol but tried to avoid letting the old man see it. He was no puritan but as the product of alcoholics, and with some problems of his own way back when, he hated to see them turning to booze in times of crisis, afraid it would become a habitual response to troubles. And for some, it had. And of course the old man *knew* that it wasn't always coffee people were sipping from one of his chipped mugs. Likewise, he knew that he was dying, though he claimed he wasn't, and had accepted hospice only when told it was the only way to get that jazzy hospital bed for the living room. And because he had cheated death so many times before, a Klan bullet in North Carolina that tore through the bedroom wall, an intentional car wreck with the first wife he was loathe to talk about, they all believed it was *possible* that he might wake up one morning, stretch, and climb out of bed for another year, another decade.

At Thanksgiving, his father's house had been filled with pilgrims who'd made their way from Minnesota, Nebraska, New Mexico, Montana, both Dakotas. It had fallen to Larsen to prepare the dinner, all of it, a big turkey, a ham, garlic mashed potatoes, green bean casserole, oyster stuffing, the works. He had been doing all the cooking since arriving in Idaho, and nobody seemed interested in helping him, but the truth was, he liked having a way to keep busy. When everyone fled to avoid doing the dishes, going off to the mall to Christmas shop, or downstairs to watch football and nap, or out to the garage to drink beer, he took a break from cleaning up to sit by his father. He watched the old man fumbling with his pipe. Even the muscle memory of something he'd been doing for decades wasn't strong enough to overcome his recalcitrant body, his stiff and hooked fingers. Larsen gently took the pipe from him. Added some Borkum-Riff tobacco, tamped it down. His father laughed. "Remember when you used light my pipe for me when I was driving on our long trips?"

"Of course," Larsen said. "It's what got me into smoking at a very young age. Thank you." He struck a wooden kitchen match and lighted the pipe, taking long, even puffs, until the coals were alive. Handed it back to his father carefully, like in some ancient ritual, waiting until he had a firm grip on the bowl. Larsen tilted his head and watched the smoke curling up toward the ceiling, yellowed from years of pipe smoke. They would have to paint that, he thought, when they eventually sold the house, in the usual tradition of removing every trace of those who had lived there. He imagined leaving the smoke stains, along with a little plaque, like Hemingway's roped-off bar stool at La Floridita in Havana.

His father waved his pipe back and forth. "There's probably material for a novel around here. Or at least a short story."

"At least." Larsen had reached over to spread the blanket over his father's bare legs. They were scaly and black, like trees from some sinister forest in a Grimm's fairy tale. They scared the children, ruined appetites.

His father took a long, thoughtful puff. "Well," he said. "I'm sure you'll know what to leave in and what to leave out."

Larsen shrugged, uneasy. His father was one of those people who seemed to never speak impulsively, so he felt like something was about to be expected of him. His father had already revised his will, which read like some kind of ornately-languaged proclamation posted to a fiefdom gate by an ambitious lord. The house, for example, had to remain in the family as long as his sister wanted to continue living there, and it had to remain painted turquoise blue, with no variation, not robin's egg blue or sky blue. The house had the look of something you might find in Key West, fitting for its placement on a street called Mar Vista. Larsen had no idea who had named the street Mar Vista, but it seemed to come from a place of unfulfilled dreams. Mar Vista meant *ocean view*, but the Pacific was at least seven hundred miles west. The actual view was of a scrubby, brown hillside where instead of a fringe of surf you might see the occasional mangy coyote weaving his way through the sagebrush. Larsen's mother had claimed the old man bought the house entirely because of the name of the street, that smaller houses more suited to a retired couple were available close by. The logical question was why his father had not simply moved to a place with an actual view of the ocean, but he was not known for doing the obvious. Maybe it was because he had an affinity for the contrary. He ran several email discussion lists but still used an old manual typewriter. All of his heroes were mavericks: Big Bill Haywood, John Reed, Zapata, Geronimo, Elizabeth Gurley Flynn. In any event, the house would stay turquoise. His will demanded that his cats be cared for with regular visits to the veterinarian, with no expense spared. None of his descendants could ever attend the three universities the old man had taught for, all of which he believed had shafted him. That kind of thing, and because he really couldn't control much of what might happen down the line, there was an explicit threat of poltergeist-style hauntings if these wishes were not acted upon. The will was vague where it should not have been, as with his retirement funds, but very particular when it came to the most ordinary possessions, like his ancient, greasy Stetson, a remnant of his youth as an Arizona cowboy, and a certain Kennedy half-dollar.

"With fiction," his father said, "there's always room for denial, isn't there?"

"I suppose so," Larsen said. "They say all writing is autobiographical, but you never know for sure how close to the truth a story comes."

Somewhere in the house, a child had laughed and another child screamed. A panicked cat burst into the room, scaled the heavy curtains, and leapt to the top of a high bookshelf. A little bronze bust of Lenin toppled and fell to the floor. "What the hell," his father said. "If that's the case, then leave it all in."

Purple Sage

ALL IT TAKES TO CARVE a carrot into a flower are a few diagonal cuts around the surface, not quite to the center. The top is twisted away, and what remains should look sort of like a rose. Blake learned how to do this while watching a string of home decorating programs on television. When he was bedridden, suffering a mysterious ailment that left him fatigued and coughing, he learned how, at least in theory, to cover light switch plates with wallpaper, fashion faux bamboo from cardboard paper towel rolls, and turn ordinary food into festive decorations.

Now with the party only four days away, Blake stood over the kitchen sink with a bag of carrots and a paring knife, attempting the flowers for the first time. He carved a few, eating the rejects, until he got the hang of it. They weren't half-bad, he decided, and he carried one outside to the back yard where his wife was tending to her flowers. He waited until Rae emptied the watering can before handing her the carrot. "What do you think?"

She regarded the carrot in her muddy palm. "What kind of flower is it supposed to be?"

"I don't know. It just sort of represents a flower. But I think it looks like a rose."

"No, it doesn't. Not a rose."

"Do we want these at the party?"

"Do we?"

Blake plucked the carrot from her hand and held it up to her face, eye level. He rotated the carrot like it was a volume dial. "Might be nice," he said. "We could garnish the coleslaw with them. Poke them in around the edges?"

"It's an idea," Rae said. She started for the house, the faucet. "What I really need you to do is go to town and get oil for the Tiki torches."

When her back was turned, he dropped the carrot into the marigolds, where it almost blended in. "Okay," he said. "Do we need anything else? As long as I'm in town?"

"Do you want to get your costume?"

"I still haven't decided what I want to be." He hurried to catch up with her. "But I've been leaning toward a spaceman."

"A spaceman? What are you talking about?"

"The old sixties television spaceman, that kind of spaceman. I thought I could get one of those silver blankets, those reflective silver blankets, you know? And then a welding helmet."

She reached down and slapped her calf. A mosquito exploded into a star of blood. "Goddamn," she said. "That reminds me. Get some of that bug killing stuff."

"Tempo? If I can find it. It's hard to find right now."

"We're going to have to do something before the party."

"What do you think? About the spaceman?"

"Do what you want, but that would be like wearing a sauna. My dad had one of those helmets. Those helmets are lined with asbestos."

He drove to Fargo on narrow roads, between sprawling green sugar beet fields. The beets were growing fast now, making themselves more valuable before harvest. They'd be collected and mashed and refined and turned into white granulated sugar in café packets and ten-pound sacks. As a teenager, Blake once picked up a beet from the road after it had fallen from a truck and hurled it against the asphalt to break it open and tasted one of the pieces. Not sweet. The whole processing concept was a mystery to him, even though he'd lived in these parts since he was fifteen. Until then, he'd assumed all sugar came from Hawaiian cane. On the very rare occasion that company arrived from elsewhere in the country, Blake liked taking detours that led past the piling sites with their mountains of sugar beets, or past the big plant in Moorhead where the actual alchemy took place, and explain, ad-libbing when necessary, how important the Red River Valley was to the rest of the world. You couldn't do that with grain because grain was kind of abstract, only an ingredient, but everyone understood sugar, even children. "This is a sugar factory," he'd say, as they rolled past the sprawling complex shooting thick steam into the sky. It was, frankly, the most interesting thing in the area to look at.

The hardware store had Tiki torch oil but not Tempo. The clerk suggested Gun World, of all places. Blake couldn't imagine why a sporting goods store would have mosquito killer, but then again, everyone seemed to be diversifying in order to survive. The only independent bookstore left in Fargo still had the best selection of books, but they also sold tin toys and fancy soap as well. So he drove to Gun World. He'd never been there before. He wasn't a hunter although he owned a deer rifle, a bulky Marlin .30-30 handed down to him by his father, who now lived alone in Mobile, Alabama and liked to send frequent postcards with no message other than the temperature, like coded intelligence dispatches. It seemed like a waste of a stamp to Blake, but if his father was trying to make him jealous on a bleak thirty-below day with a cheerful "seventy-nine!" on the reverse of a card showing the sun setting into the ocean, well, it was working.

He roamed the store. Everyone employed there wore blaze-orange t-shirts and seemed trained to hurl themselves into the aisles and greet customers. There was something vaguely cult-like about their smiling eyes, reminding Blake in a heart-breaking sort of way of his trip to San Francisco many years earlier, before he was married, when he wandered around Fisherman's Wharf and encountered some Hare Krishnas. If you added hair and orange shirts, they were now working at Gun World. Blake tried to walk fast and look like he knew what he was doing, but after one loop through the store, he couldn't find the Tempo and had to ask and then had to endure a banal conversation about the relative size of mosquitos in the northern plains versus back east. And so on. He scooped ten packets of the deadly powder from a giant barrel and started for the cash registers, passing racks of alert rifles and shotguns, pistols in glass cases, camouflage clothing, duck calls.

He was amazed at how many products were available to help people pursue their hobbies. He had never really had a hobby, though for a time he'd been very interested in photography. Blake had wanted to shoot dramatic, heart-clutching landscapes in the tradition of Ansel Adams and Galen Rowell, or powerful glimpses of humanity like Dorothea Lange, but his efforts, even with a five hundred dollar Nikon, were always disappointing—snapshots and not art. Driving home once on Highway 10 in the early spring, he'd spotted the remains of a deer emerging from a melting snowbank, ribs jutting toward the gray sky, and he'd gone for the camera and returned, set up his tripod on the shoulder, shot from different angles, but the resulting photographs looked less like art than dinner scraps thrown onto dirty snow, and he'd never really tried again.

A display of antique firearms caught his eye. There was a *Quigley Down Under* movie poster in the case, hanging behind a long Sharps rifle. "Own my gun," someone had written in black marker on a paper balloon venturing from Tom Selleck's mouth. There were old Winchester lever action rifles with brittle-looking stocks as well. He was kneeling to examine what a sign identified as an 1851 Colt Navy revolver reproduction with a surprisingly low price tag of two hundred dollars when an orange shirt rose from behind the case as if on an elevator. "That's a real buy, if you're looking at that Colt."

"I can see that."

"The fellow who owned it only fired maybe a dozen balls through it, and he was real meticulous about keeping her clean, which you have to be with black powder."

"You mean it actually shoots? It says *reproduction*."

"Oh yes. Reproduction as opposed to *antique*. Actually, these re-pops are better than the originals because steel is better now. Technology and all that. Do you want to handle it?"

Blake did but feared the same sort of high pressure you gathered when agreeing to test-drive a car. He was conjuring an escape line when the clerk simply slid open the glass door and removed the revolver and handed it to Blake, butt first. "Check the balance."

"Well, just for a second." He gripped the revolver and aimed it vaguely at the clerk's groin. The clerk pretended not to notice, in the manner of a good waiter being smothered in a cloud of cigar smoke while taking an order. "This is nice," Blake said.

"Let me tell you something. Wild Bill Hickok used an 1851 like this, and he kept on using it even after everyone else was using cartridge revolvers. That's how sweet a piece it was. Have you ever shot black powder?"

"Not really. No." Blake inspected the revolver. The cylinder bore a naval battle scene.

"You're missing out on a whole lot of fun, then."

"How does it work?"

The clerk smiled and took the revolver from Blake and worked the loading lever under the barrel. A plunger disappeared into one of the chambers in the cylinder. Blake was fascinated now. He admired feats of engineering, small and huge. His mind was still reeling after watching a documentary on the Panama Canal.

"You drop in some powder, then you seat a ball and lever it down real tight, and that's all she wrote. Cover it with some grease, put a cap on the nipple, and she's ready to rock."

"Cap?"

"Percussion cap." The clerk assumed a Hollywood Indian voice. "Cap blow fire through nipple, start heap big fire in chamber. Make ball go like thunder." He laughed. "It's a lot of fun, like I said."

Blake took the revolver from him. Pulled back the hammer and put a mounted caribou head in the sights. "Can you get blanks for this?"

"Well, you could just fire it with some powder and grease packed in. But you could hurt somebody still. That stuff flying out at a million miles an hour. That could smart."

Blake nodded, let the hammer down. He imagined being at the party, Rae's friends and coworkers from the postal service nervously eyeballing the revolver. *Is that thing real?*

Hell yes, it's real.

Is that appropriate?

"I'll take it," Blake said. "Give me some powder and whatnot, too."

"Do you need a powder measure and flask?"

"Whatever."

"Balls?"

"Everything."

He wanted a hat but found at the western store in the mall that a new cowboy hat would set him back well over a hundred dollars. Rae had not given him a budget for his costume, but he was pretty sure a hundred dollar hat, along with the revolver, would be over the top. Rae was going as Laverne from *Laverne and Shirley,* and her sister was getting decked out as Shirley. Toni's husband was going to be Squiggy. So of course they'd wanted Blake to be Lenny, and his refusal had been another notch in the paddle they believed he was using to head up the river of intransigence. But even Rae softened a little, agreeing that while Squiggy had a trademark leather jacket and curly greased hair, Lenny was pretty boring, the straight man, more or less, of the duo. And whereas Toni's husband Carl, with a background in college theatre, was getting into the Squiggy role to the point of trying to gain weight, Blake had no interest in method acting a supporting role from a program that, even in his youth, in the late seventies, had struck him as utterly banal. For a costume he'd considered and rejected a bunch of concepts: a Viking outfit would be too hot if done correctly, and he ran the risk of having other Vikings at the party, given the football team in Minneapolis and widely Scandinavian heritage of their guests. George Armstrong Custer, with arrows poking from a special vest he wasted an afternoon designing, had, after thinking about it, seemed a little insensitive, especially since one of their guests would likely be Craig Elk Nation, a Native American mail carrier. Then the spaceman, passive-aggressively vetoed by Rae. But a cowboy was perfect, because he could protect his head from the harsh sun with a hat, get away with not shaving for a couple of days to add a fresh from the trail look, and perhaps even carry a bottle of whisky and drink from it. He went across town to the biggest thrift store in the area and, in Shoes and Hats, found not a cowboy hat but something close, a giant sombrero festooned with red velvet and tiny mirrors. It was a little pricey for a thrift store at twenty dollars but could stand as a wall decoration if needed after the party. Anyway, he tried it on, and the sombrero fit. Now he was a *vaquero*. They did not have a holster, but he found a very wide tooled belt with the name *Larry* stamped across the back. He could just stick the revolver into the belt and let it go at that. He already owned a red shirt with a lime green cactus print. He had jeans, of course, and ostrich cowboy boots he hadn't worn since his single days. He was set. Out in the parking lot he tried on the sombrero again. At noon, the sun was high, but he was instantly bathed in protective shade, which, when he stood perfectly upright, created a perfect circle around his feet. In a pleasantly simple epiphany, he understood the rationale behind the sombrero, the equation of heat and sun and exposed field workers, and also recalled the little ceramic "Juan" in his grandmother's back yard, dozing under a sombrero while weeds sprang up around him.

He looked up from the shade to see a Mexican woman striding toward him. She wasn't an apparition; in her hand was a garbage bag, and she averted her eyes but passed closely enough that he could see a fine sheen of perspiration on her high forehead. He turned and watched her swing the bag and throw it a good twenty feet into a dumpster. "Two points," Blake said.

She cocked her head. "Pardon me?"

"Nothing. A joke."

She reached up and lifted the sombrero from his head, turned it around, set it back down. "Better," she said.

"Muchas gracias."

"You speak?"

"No. Not really."

She laughed. Walked back to the thrift store, to the bay doors where people dropped off sacks of clothing and household junk faster than the employees could process them for resale. She wore white sweatbands on her wrists. When she reached the door, she looked back and gave him a little wave.

He called Rae. It was enough of a nuisance to go ten miles to town that checking in before heading home was prudent. He tended to forget things, and a phone call had preempted a cool reception more than once.

"I found the Tempo," he said. "Christ that stuff is expensive."

"Well, we need it. What about the Tiki torch oil?"

"Check. I found my costume."

"Oh? What is it?"

"A surprise."

"Come on. You know I don't like surprises. It's the spaceman, isn't it? Tell me."

"It's not the spaceman. It is historical, kind of."

"Oh Jesus. Listen, Toni just called. My Laverne wig came in. She's got clients today, so she can't bring it out. Can you swing by and pick it up?"

"You can't do it?"

"Please? I'm cleaning to beat heck, and if I stop, I'll lose my motivation. I even got the fridge pulled out. You should see how gross it is under there."

"I'll get the wig."

Toni and Carl lived in south Moorhead, right on the Red River. Their back yard sloped sharply to the water, almost forty-five degrees, but during the 1997 flood, the river made it up to the patio doors and lapped against the glass. At the time, Toni was recovering from a broken wrist and Carl was too hysterical to be of much use, so Blake and Rae had helped build a semi-circular wall of sandbags. A busload of volunteers showed up in the neighborhood, including a small band of black-cloaked, bearded men from the Hutterite colony, who'd enjoyed heaving sandbags at Blake and watching him try to keep up with their fast pace. Now, years later, his shoulder still occasionally hurt from it.

Toni was in between clients. She had a secondary school teaching certificate but made vastly more money using an electronic unit to remove unwanted hair. The living room at Toni and Carl's doubled as her studio. There was always some form of aromatherapy occurring. Today the room smelled of mangos, though Blake would not have identified the odor if Toni hadn't seen him sniffing and announced, "Mellow Mango."

"Ah."

She glanced at her watch. "My two-thirty is very ticklish. Mango for some reason makes people less sensitive to that kind of thing. But the jury's still out. I haven't tried it yet."

"Rae said something about a wig?"

"Yes." Toni reached into a cardboard box atop her prized antique sideboard. He caught a glimpse of glossy black leather when she pulled out the blond wig, and when Toni faced him again, she was a little flustered, hurrying to pull on the wig and clown around for a moment. He wanted to know what the black leather was all about.

Blake and Toni had always flirted playfully a bit around others, but when confined alone, some awkwardness arose. Still, he had time while watching her goof around to entertain a brief fantasy in which the leather was a dominatrix outfit, Toni offering to model it for him.

What about your two-thirty client?

You're it, bad boy.

"Tell Rae she'll need to hang and brush it. When they're new, there's always some sort of a coating on them." She removed the wig and held it up on one hand, ran her fingers down the hair, formed it into a ponytail. "I don't suppose she has a wig head."

"I don't think so."

"Then you can use, like, a beach ball? Only don't inflate it all the way."

"Gotcha."

She handed him the wig. Blake tucked it under his arm and stroked it like a puppy. Toni stared at the wig. Blake regarded his sister-in-law's fleshy arms and tan neck. Sometimes he felt like making a bold move, grabbing her, kissing her, gambling that she would reciprocate, and a new and exotic season would open up in his life, the way new refugees from Somalia could be seen silhouetted against their first snowfall in Fargo, frolicking in what the locals considered a nuisance. But if he ever played that card and it was the wrong card, the repercussions could be pretty serious. Blood was thicker than water.

"Say," she said. "Did you decide what to be? For the party?"

"Yes, but I'm keeping it a secret."

"What, you want to make some kind of grand entrance?"

"Nope."

"Afraid she'll shoot it down?"

"Rae? Never."

Toni laughed. "You better run along. I have to get ready for this bikini job."

"I can't watch?"

"It's not as sexy as it sounds."

"Let me hit your restroom and me and this hair will get out of your hair."

"Ha ha."

Blake lifted the seat and urinated though not urgently. The men in his family had been blessed with healthy bladders. He could certainly have made it another twenty minutes until he was back home.

But Blake was looking for something, and while the flush camouflaged his act, he slid open the medicine cabinet and scanned the shelves. While ill, he had developed what he considered not an addiction to but an *enthusiasm* for Lortab, Vicodin, Tylenol 3, Codeine. The resident he saw at the walk-in clinic had cheerfully prescribed a two-week's supply of Lortab to help Blake get some relief from nights spent coughing and jerking. This was before Blake concluded that mold in the basement was the problem, before he stripped all the old ceiling tiles, painted Kilz primer over the beams, and purchased a huge Honeywell air cleaner to purify his environment. The Lortab had worked, though, and he'd found that it gave him a sort of lucid buzz, a mellowing. Rae had made the mistake of mentioning that her sister had been prescribed Vicodin for something, stomach cramps perhaps, but didn't like taking them because they weren't natural. Now Blake studied each label in the cabinet. Evidently Carl was experimenting with herbal "performance enhancers," something called *Cobra*, and a liquid Muira Puama. Blake screwed up his face. Carl had always struck him as a bit on the perverted side. Then he saw the Vicodin and hefted the bottle. Opened it and looked inside. It was full. Just sitting there. He had intended on taking only a few but dropped the whole bottle into his pocket and spread things out on the shelf to fill in the gap. He hoped that one of Toni's clients would be blamed.

Later, Rae appeared in the doorway of Blake's home office. Her face was slick with sweat and her hands were speckled with redwood deck stain. "Working hard?" she asked.

"What do you need me to do?"

"You could help me a little. We've got like three days only."

"We're ahead of the game. At least compared to last time."

She started crying. Little baby sniffles. Rare for her.

"Now what's wrong?"

She came in and pushed aside the magazines and books on Blake's old green loveseat and perched on the edge. Sighed and scraped at her stained palms with her fingernails. "I'm just afraid it'll be a dud party like last time."

He swiveled in his chair. He'd been reading about Wild Bill Hickok in a giant PBS series companion book about The West. When his mother gave him the book for Christmas, he'd thought it was just more schlock but now found it pretty interesting and thorough. "Okay," he said. "It won't be a dud. We've got the whole costume thing happening this year. And that new pig man you found is supposed to be the best."

"He better be. He's costing us twice what we paid last time."

"And remember last time it was cloudy and gloomy. All the weathermen are saying nothing but sunshine this weekend."

"What if they're wrong? Maybe costumes are a bad idea. People don't want to have to *plan* when they go to a party. They just want to go."

"Everyone we've talked to is looking forward to it. Your sister is pretty stoked about it."

"I wish you'd tell me what you're going to be."

"No can do."

She scratched her bare knee and stood. "Can you spray for mosquitoes? I barely got started on the stupid deck and they were eating me alive. I had to stop."

"I can do that."

Fifteen minutes later, Blake emerged from the house wearing wraparound NASCAR shades and elbow-high rubber gloves. He knelt in the front yard with a packet of Tempo and the sprayer. Mosquitoes zeroed in on his cheeks, the back of his neck. He whipped himself with the glove and then shook powder into the sprayer, filled the unit with water from the hose. Glanced around the neighborhood. No children were out playing. The mosquitoes had not been bad at all that summer, and then, after a week of heavy rain that left warm, standing pools in the farm fields and depressions in yards, they sprang to life, hungry and focused. The authorities in their little town released a fog late at night from the bed of a pickup, but it only seemed to enrage the mosquitoes. When Blake had taken a letter to the mailbox the evening before, he'd felt the mosquitoes like raindrops on his swinging arms and had bolted in a Hitchcock-style panic. Now he screwed down the top of the sprayer and pumped the handle to build up pressure for the wand.

He went to the back yard and started coating the lilacs, the trees, and the dark earth underneath the deck. Mosquitoes came up in whirling clouds and hid again in the leaves. One made a reconnaissance mission into Blake's right ear. He sprayed the cottonwood trunks. He recalled that at one time, he'd been dead set against any and all poison, whether for bugs or weeds. He'd been on an all-natural kick. He had ordered a brochure on organic beef and tried to talk Carl and Toni into splitting a cow.

Rae had brought in softball-sized stones to line the flowerbeds, and Blake sprayed the cracks between them. Back in the front yard, he reloaded the sprayer and began making passes across the lawn. He spotted his wife's pale face in the window, watching him as she rubbed lotion into her hands and forearms. She suffered from chronically dry skin. To caress her was to caress exterior-grade plywood. Blake had once playfully rubbed Toni's back at the lake, had marveled at how smooth her skin was, like a warm ball of pizza dough. God had divided things up in strange ways with those two. Rae owned a slim figure while Toni was husky; Rae's hands were delicate while Toni's were large with slightly crooked fingers. Toni moved like one of the big African cats, a lioness, maybe, with a grace that belied her bulky frame. Rae's interior anxieties seemed to propel her with quick, jerky motions. She had given birth to an equally pasty, nervous child, their daughter Lucinda, who was still undecided about whether or not to drive down from college in Crookston for the party because she feared a tornado might bear down on her car, out in the middle of nowhere, with no hills, no buildings, only shallow interstate ditches to hide in. Rae was trying to get Blake to "run up" to Crookston to get their daughter, but so far he'd refused, claiming the need for "tough love" to help Lucinda escape the stranglehold of irrational fear.

In the garage, he peeled off the gloves and draped them over the sprayer handle. Removed his sunglasses. Went inside and washed his hands and face, picked dead mosquitoes from his nape. He wasn't especially hungry, but Rae had whipped up a colorful pasta and pepperoni salad, a new recipe she was considering for the party. She scooped a bowlful for him and watched him eat it, hands on her hips. "What's the wet stuff?" he asked.

"Italian salad dressing. Low fat."

"This is good," he said.

"Just good or real good?"

"It's great. It's a taste sensation, I'd say."

"You have to be honest. I don't want to make a huge bowlful and have it just sit there like my pretzels did last time."

"I liked the pretzels." She'd coated them with butter-flavored popcorn oil, garlic powder, dill. Blake had been glad for the leftovers.

"Nobody else did."

"They probably thought the pretzels were just *regular* pretzels. You should have advertised them somehow."

"Well, I can't do everything. You could have quote advertised them unquote. You saw them just sitting on the table getting ignored."

"Can we talk about something else?"

"What else is there? Blake, in three days we're going to have— knock on wood—dozens of people wandering around here. We're running out of time."

"We're not running out of time."

"So is that okay? Should I make it for Saturday?"

"By all means."

"Then I have to go shopping." His wife pulled her ongoing shopping list from under a refrigerator magnet. Patted her hair. "Do I look okay for the store?"

"Yes."

He followed her out to the driveway. Her head swiveled. Left to right, up and down. She pointed at the light pole on the corner of their property. "Make sure when you mow the lawn you get that long grass over there."

He nodded. She climbed into her Cherokee and turned up the music. Blake wandered out to the back yard. No mosquitoes leaped out to attack. He shook the lilac bush. No angry little cloud emerged. But there were no birds singing on the wire or in the trees, either, as if they sensed the chemical danger. No squirrels. Blake couldn't detect any life at all.

When he was sure Rae wouldn't be coming back to check the cupboard or grab a new booklet of blank checks, Blake opened the trunk and removed the sombrero and bag from Gun World. He hurried inside and locked the door and sat at the kitchen table and examined the revolver again. Aimed it at the cat, who slid from her perch on the chair and flitted down the hall. He opened a can of black powder, sniffed it, poured a few grains into his palm, then blew them into the air. Hefted one of the .36 caliber lead balls. "These could do some damage," he whispered.

He strapped on the belt, dropped the sombrero onto his head. Stuck the revolver into the belt in a cross-draw fashion. In the bedroom, before the big mirror over the dresser, Blake regarded the transformation. He looked a little scary. He rested his hand on the revolver butt, stared himself down, and drew the pistol. There was an awfully long gap between the time he drew it and when he was able to cock the hammer. Long enough to lose a gunfight for sure. He glared at his reflection. "You, sir, are a loser. You are middle-aged, living in Minnesota. You own three televisions. Conversations with your friends and neighbors are nothing more than bumper-sticker dialogue. Upon your death there will be an inch of particulars in the *Fargo Forum*, which your wife will clip and paste into her scrapbook along with a photo of you, in front of the lake, holding a fishing rod but no fish."

There was a moment, he discovered, after taking a Vicodin, when things seemed to be going along normally, and then an almost audible *click* would happen and his mind would stop reeling, his aches and thick lungs would ease, his thoughts would simplify. A certain giddiness would creep in. It usually happened after about a half hour or so, depending on when he'd eaten, how much coffee he'd consumed, how stressful his day had been, what the pollen levels were. And then upon going to bed, his dreams were interesting, and he'd rise early and energetic having captured a solid night's sleep.

After Rae went to bed, Blake swallowed one of the pilfered pills and sat at his desk, reading more of the old west book. He held the revolver in his lap. He found its weight comforting. The Vicodin kicked in, and he spent a half hour looking at a single photograph of a mountain of buffalo skulls. The photo looked abstract until he bent close and made a point of examining individual skulls. Each a separate being. Each born on wobbly legs before learning to graze and charge and couple. Maybe they didn't mind sacrificing themselves now and then to sustain the Indians, fill the bellies of laughing brown children, break the wind against a tipi in December, have their horns grace a chief's head. Be rolled on by a muscular twenty-year-old and his bride. Any moron, Blake decided, even among the buffalo, would choose that sacrifice over watching hundreds of his own drop at the hands of calculating, armed white men shooting from railroad cars. Not in this book but somewhere, Blake had heard about thousands of rotting carcasses stinking up the plains because the meat was deemed worthless as opposed to the hides. The rifle barrels grew so hot from making countless shots that hunters would urinate into the muzzles to cool the steel. Even with the blessing of codeine, the buffalo were beginning to depress Blake, and he shut the book, cocked the revolver, let the hammer down, cocked it again. Right-handed, left-handed. As sometimes happened with the codeine, items in his peripheral vision started to move. His coffee cup began to slide as if he were on a ship in rolling seas. This was the optimum time to hit the sack and maybe have a good dream.

Rae had reserved a 20x40 foot canopy from the rental outfit in Moorhead. They'd used one for their last party, and although it didn't rain, just having it alleviated anxiety. So it was worth the exorbitant cost.

The warehouse helper was a meth-head in a Metallica shirt. "So what are you having, a wedding?"

"Pig roast."

"Oh, man, I love a good pig roast. You got sauce?"

"There will be sauce." Blake watched the man lift folding chairs and muscle them to the trailer attached to Blake's pickup. The man had spindly arms covered with outrageous tattoos of dragons and clowns, all poorly executed.

"I think the sauce can make or break the meat, you know what I'm saying? Like, if you have good meat and some of that shitty sauce, that shit in the plastic bottles, you know what I'm saying? I hope you have some good sauce."

"The pig man brings the sauce," Blake said. He was trying to count the chairs without being too obvious about it.

"What to drink, man? Beer, I hope. You can't have a pig without beer."

"There will be beer."

"Keg or bottle?"

"Keg."

"No thanks, then, none of that piss for me. What are we up to on chairs?"

"Thirty-seven, I think."

The meth-head counted off thirteen more chairs and stacked them in the trailer and regarded the long column. "Lot of chairs."

"We're expecting a lot of people."

"Family?"

Blake shook his head and wondered, as he often did, if there was something about his face that made him more approachable than, say, Rae, who always elicited from strangers only the barest riggings of conversation. It amazed him because he wasn't a natural smiler either and tended to wear a deadpan expression most of the time. Maybe it was in the eyes, he thought, watching the meth-head grab the heavy canvas sack containing the canopy and dance it in circles over the concrete floor. Sunglasses, he decided. Next time he'd try sunglasses.

Setting up the canopy was supposed to be a matter of starting the side poles and raising the three center poles. Then a little adjusting and tightening with stakes and guy lines. But it didn't quite work out that way. The tent collapsed, and Blake found himself trapped under what seemed like an acre of heavy, vinyl-coated canvas. He was hot and sweaty and bitter about all the guests who would take this, take all of it, for granted. He and Rae shelled out quite a bit for these shindigs. They refused the twenty dollar bills offered by some of the more conscientious guests or the offers to bring food. They both believed it was tacky to do otherwise. They liked the idea of providing a merry day and doing it with what Rae believed was *class* with a capital C.

Late in the afternoon, Blake stood before a mountain of discarded tree limbs, heaps of mulch, a few illegally dumped tires on the edge of town. The Colt was loaded, the act performed on the car hood with the powder can weighting the Xeroxed instructions the clerk at Gun World had given him. You had to focus because if a double load of powder was dropped into one of the cylinders, the gun could explode and send strips of steel into eye, heart, testicle. Likewise, if you didn't cover each cylinder hole with a plug of mucous-like grease, a chain reaction firing could start with similarly tragic results. "I'd venture to say a lot of civil war causalities were from a soldier's own gun going haywire," the Gun World clerk had said. "Can you imagine going off to war and your own revolver kills you?"

"That would be ironic."

"It would flat out suck."

Now he cocked the revolver and raised it elegantly from his side. He aimed at a weathered split-wood fence post someone had snuck onto the pile. Pulled the trigger. There was a snap that made him flinch but no report. He tried again and again; nothing happened. He turned the revolver around to inspect the cylinder until he realized he was aiming a loaded gun at his face. He hurried to the car to look at the instructions and realized he'd forgotten the percussion caps.

"Ah," he said.

When he pulled the trigger the next time, there was a loud report, though not the rude explosion of the .357 his father had once let him fire. White smoke flowed from the muzzle. The gun did not buck in his hand like Dad's Smith & Wesson, which had left his teenaged palm feeling like he'd tried to hammer a nail into concrete. But he didn't hit the target, either. The ball disappeared into a tangle of yard waste branches. He cocked the revolver and moved closer, to within ten feet, and this time a hole appeared in the post, though not close to the headwaters of the crack he'd been aiming at. No matter. He shot again, instinctively from the hip, and this time hit the crack. "I have a gift," he said. "Me and Bill Hickok."

Rae was on the telephone, ordering a portable toilet. She was in the Laverne outfit, the sweater with the monogrammed *L* over her left breast, which seemed larger than usual. Hair from her light brown wig hung down to the yellow legal pad she was writing on. This temporary stranger was asking if the portable toilet included a urinal and if it was wide enough to accommodate "sloppy visitors."

"Uh-huh," she said. She glanced up and rolled her eyes at Blake. "Well, as long as it won't like *reek* if it's here for a couple extra days, then Tuesday will be okay to pick it up."

She hung up and whipped her hair back. "I thought I had capris like Laverne wore, but I don't. I don't know what happened to them. All I have are some stupid culottes from like 1980 or something."

"Do they still fit?"

"Do they still fit? What kind of question is that? Of course they still fit. Almost. But that's irrelevant, because Laverne didn't wear culottes, she wore capris. How about the sweater? What do you think?"

"Sexy. Really accentuates the positive."

"You dope, I stuffed my bra." She started to reach under the sweater. "And they itch."

Blake grabbed her wrist. "Wait."

"For what? Let go."

"Leave them in." He tried to kiss her.

"I said they *itch*, Blake. Now cut it out."

"Come on. Please?"

"No means no. Besides, you reek. What have you been doing, anyway? You smell like rotten eggs."

The sulfur from the black powder. He backed away a little. His wife's nose was twitching like a rabbit's. "It's gross," she said.

Blake assumed the blank stare offered by all those hoodlums on *Cops*. "I don't smell it."

"You need a shower."

"Join me, Laverne?"

Rae reached under her sweater and dug for two handfuls of green Easter grass. "This stuff has got to go."

"You used Easter grass?"

"What would you have used?"

"I don't know. Styrofoam?"

She handed him her grassy breasts. "Toss these for me."

He brought them to his nose and inhaled.

"Pig," she said.

The Vicodin didn't make Blake sleepy, not for the first couple hours after taking it, anyway. He was pretty sure it had something to do with feeling so good that he *wanted* to be awake. Even after buying the air cleaner and removing anything in the basement that could harbor mold, he was still prone to bouts of congestion and muscle aches. Rae had been skeptical about the basement's role in his illness. She didn't have a problem, after all. She thought it was a genetic issue, even though nobody in his family recalled such an affliction among their own. His father counseled him to move to the desert. Blake tried to imagine the dry air, nights with the window open and his lungs as clean as a Finn's kitchen. Long, deep breaths, in and out, for eight hours. It was unfathomable, like trying to imagine an acid trip from a description in a novel. He would not have minded pulling up stakes and heading for the desert. He saw an endless field of sagebrush, maybe purple sage if there truly was such a thing, and dark red peppers hanging from a string on the wall. But Rae was anchored to Minnesota. She'd already bought their burial plots.

He adjusted his sombrero in the bathroom mirror. The hat nearly touched the walls, it was that big around. He tried pushing it back in a more casual manner, but the result was more comical than anything else, like some bandit in an old television western—*The Rifleman*, maybe. Pulled down low, the brim became a blindfold. What seemed to work best was the way the Mexican woman at the thrift store had cocked it a bit to the side after putting it on him. He recalled the muscles in her forearms bulging from under the white sweatbands. There was something familiar about her, but he couldn't put his finger on it until the Vicodin kicked in and his mind opened up. "La buena fama durmiendo," he suddenly thought. He knelt by the closet door and rummaged through his photography supplies until he found his old issues of *Camera and Darkroom*. He carried the magazines to the desk and pushed aside the PBS book. The sombrero stole the light and he spun it like a Frisbee to the loveseat.

He found the article on Manuel Álvarez Bravo and then "La Buena Fama Durmiendo," the photograph of a Mexican girl on her back, her ankles wrapped in white—not sweatbands, but that was the connection, he thought, to the woman at the thrift store. The girl was nude from the waist up, young enough to have breasts that remained alert even while prone. Her eyes were closed, and cacti of some sort were arranged around her. "Good Reputation Sleeping" was the title translation offered. Blake couldn't figure out whether or not the girl was supposed to be sleeping the sleep of the dead or just plain sleeping. He wished he knew. It felt important to know.

Voices in the kitchen roused him from sleep. Cupboards opening and closing. Water running. Rae and Toni were making potato salad. Blake tied his bathrobe and stumbled in, poured a cup of coffee, and dodged a steaming kettle of boiling potatoes Toni was rushing to the sink. His wife spun around from the counter, and the blade of her Chicago Cutlery butcher knife came within inches of eviscerating him. She didn't seem to notice. "I have potholders, you know," she said to Toni.

"I'm okay. Ouch."

"Good morning, all," Blake said.

"Get dressed and take that coffee to go," Rae said.

He roamed Wal-Mart, working from Rae's last minute list. *Serving spoon. Wet wipes. Aluminum foil, thick!* He grabbed the most expensive roll he could find, remembering the cheap foil from last time, ripping when Rae tried to wrap the big chunks of leftover pork. All her frustration over low attendance and the weather had funneled itself into complaints about the foil, and she'd thrown the hunk of pork against the wall, thrown it like a football so that from the living room, Blake had seen the pork make one complete spiral before impacting the wallpaper, leaving a magnolia-shaped pattern of grease, still visible in the right light.

Big garbage bags. He pushed the cart around the store. Everyone had a cart, shopping so eagerly it was like the carts were pulling the people, jerking them along the consumer trail. Items seemed to jump from ledges into the carts. He wanted to warn everybody to abandon their purchases and head for fresh air, but his cart tugged him to the checkout instead.

Carl was at the house, his big Suburban hogging the driveway, blocking the garage door so that Blake had to park on the street and lug his bags. He entered the house through the garage and set the bags on the kitchen counter, gleaming now from a fresh cleaning. He opened the fridge. Huge bowls of salads and whipped-cream-covered desserts populated the shelves. He heard a squeal coming from the bedroom and wandered down the hallway. Carl was in Blake's bed, between Toni and Rae. They were watching a tape of *Laverne and Shirley.* They scarcely looked up when he came into the room. He sat on the wicker chair by the window and watched for a few minutes. He turned slightly in the chair. Carl was packed pretty tightly between the girls. Carl's left hand was wedged between his thigh and Rae's bare thigh. She had to feel his knuckles, soft as they were, pushing into her leg where it left her shorts. For her part, Toni was down farther, with her head on Carl's chest. Carl glanced at Blake but only for a moment before returning his round-eyed gaze to the television.

Blake left the room. Went to his office and dropped a Vicodin and looked at the Bravo photograph again. The girl's right leg was up, bent at the knee. And her left arm was hidden behind her head. Her hips were shrouded in white linen. If the photograph was about anything, it was a mystery to Blake. And what did the cactus symbolize? He rolled up the magazine, stuck it into his back pocket, and went to the bedroom. "I have to go back to town," he said.

His wife held up her palm. "Ssshh."

"You guys look pretty comfortable."

Toni laughed. "If you were Lenny, you could join us."

He parked at the thrift store, by the drop-off doors. Watched the women sorting through a huge washing machine box full of unfolded clothing. Pants and shoes went flying every which way. Then he saw the Mexican woman using a can of Pledge and a rag on a wooden dresser. He climbed from his car and wandered to the door and stared at her until he caught her eye. He beckoned. Her brow furrowed, and she nodded at the other girls, much closer to Blake, but he shook his head and beckoned again, and she came over. She smelled of lemon. She swiped the hair from her eyes. He wasn't sure if she remembered him, but she said, "Hey, you're the hat man."

"Yes, I am."

"Do you need something, hat man?"

Blake unrolled the magazine. "I can't figure this out," he said.

She came closer, by his shoulder. He opened to the Bravo spread. "Do you know anything about this? I can't tell if she's sleeping or dead, because I know that *durmiendo* means *sleeping,* but there's an aura of death in this picture. And I'm wondering if it can mean death also."

"Why are you showing me this?"

"You seem to know your culture pretty well, like with the sombrero. Any ideas?"

"This is a naked chick."

"Forget about that part. I'm wondering about the symbolism here."

"Hey, this guy is showing me dirty pictures," she said. The two other women straightened up.

"No," Blake said. "This is art. I just have some questions."

"Get Sylvia," the woman said.

Blake backed up a few feet. An old man in a white Panama hat appeared in the doorway. "I have these telephones," he said. "They are rotary dial telephones. They still work, however. Can you use them?"

A middle-aged woman with scarred forearms, old burns, emerged. She glared at Blake, then the old man. "Which one?"

The woman pointed at Blake. "This one. He wants me to look at dirty pictures."

"What dirty pictures?"

The woman grabbed for the magazine. Blake jerked his hand back, and all she got was the cover.

"Are you some kind of pervert?" Sylvia asked.

"This is a misunderstanding," Blake said.

"Rotary dial," the old man said. "But they're very *clean* telephones."

Blake fled.

At dusk, Blake and Rae stood on the deck and surveyed the yard, the strings of Edison lights flowing down from the trees. "I think we're done," she said. "I called the beer man, and he'll bring the trailer out at nine. The pig man should be here first thing in the morning." She slapped a mosquito from her arm. "These bastards are back, too."

"I'll spray in the morning. The poison should kick in before everyone shows up."

"Lay it down heavy, then. I mean, wipe them *out.*"

He loaded the revolver at midnight, no balls, just powder and grease and percussion caps. He liked the idea of drawing the gun and firing it straight up in the manner of a movie cowboy riding into town. Of course, Rae would be shocked, as she didn't even like him sneaking across the river into North Dakota for fireworks on Independence Day, even though everyone in town did it, turning the neighborhood into a war zone while the local cops pretended not to notice.

Morning brought gusty winds but no clouds. Blake was mowing the front yard when the pig man arrived, pulling a giant cooker behind his Dodge pickup. His wife jumped from the cab and directed the pig man while he backed up the truck, shouting commands in a high, frantic voice. They disappeared behind the garage. In a few minutes, Blake smelled charcoal lighter fluid and saw smoke rising. He heard a deep throbbing and looked up to see a Harley turning the corner. It rolled past very slowly, and the man riding it regarded

Blake through mirrored shades. Blake nodded, but the rider turned away. Blake watched him continue up the street. He looked down at his pale, thin legs. He was wearing the straw golf hat he always wore when performing yard work. It struck him that he was the opposite of the man on the Harley. He wished he had been wearing the gun and sombrero when the Harley putted by. He was pretty sure the guy would have nodded back then.

And everything went off without a hitch, really. Rae had succeeded. The party was supposed to begin at one, officially, but by noon people began to stream in. The most common costume approach seemed to be nonspecific beach bum, Hawaiian shirts and leis, some of which Rae suspected of being left over from another co-worker's tropical-themed wedding a year earlier. But others were creatively cloaked. Three men, rural mail carriers, came together dressed as hookers in wigs and short skirts, though the heat drove them to lose the wigs by dinnertime. There were more cowboys than just Blake, although he noted proudly that he was the only cowboy with a real revolver and not a cap pistol. Blake had popped two of the Vicodin to mellow himself out for the long day among what were mostly Rae's people and spent most of the afternoon in his lawn chair, kind of buzzed, watching Batman make frequent trips to the portable toilet to empty what he drunkenly confessed to Blake was a "schoolgirl's bladder." Beyond the lilacs, they'd set up horseshoes, and the wigless whores played enthusiastically. Craig Elk Nation wore a loincloth and nothing more but got chilly in the evening and borrowed Blake's purple Minnesota Vikings sweatshirt. Vampires and pirates pulled chairs close together to gossip. The office floozy strutted around in a high-cut *Baywatch* swimsuit carrying a rescue float which she playfully threw at married men, jerking them close with a nylon rope when they caught it. The pig man, accurate as a clock and dressed for the part in a white apron and high chef's hat, had the meat done and chopped and laid out promptly. His wife had gotten into the spirit with a plastic pig nose.

Rae loved Blake's outfit, although she refused to believe the gun was real. "You done good, baby," she said, pressing her fake boobs, now fashioned from flour-filled balloons, against him. "Will you announce dinner?" And Blake jumped rather deftly up to a picnic table, drew the revolver, and fired it. Everyone froze. The attention was on him. He blew smoke from the muzzle.

"Chow time," he barked.

He was pleased to see so many people, for Rae's sake. The costumes jump-started conversations, and the masks seemed to dispel inhibitions, and by nine, when the sky was starting to dim, the festivities were still going strong. The younger set was dancing on the redwood deck to a hip-hop CD one of them had brought along. Laverne and Shirley and Squiggy were a real hit. Carl had Squiggy's mannerisms down pat, although the voice was annoying. The trio fell easily into scenes from the show, and most of the guests were old enough to appreciate the effort. Toni caught Blake by the beer trailer and ran her palm along his unshaven cheek. "I've never seen you looking so rough and tough," she said.

"This is the real me," Blake said. "The other me is the costume."

"Well, if I'd known *that*."

"You'd what?"

She moved in closer until he could smell her breath, strawberry margarita with a tinge of barbecue sauce. Her hand found the gun barrel in his pants. "And if I'd known you were packing *this*," she said.

He was trying to think up a good comeback when she careened away, laughing.

Blake was behind the wall of lilacs, kicking stray sand back into the horseshoe pit, when he heard a familiar throbbing. A Harley was coming up the old alley, the headlight a yellow sun growing closer. The rider turned by the shed, backed the motorcycle up a few feet, and parked by the portable toilet. Blake thought it was the same man from that morning. He recalled the unreciprocated nod and felt a bit irritated.

The biker stretched and regarded his Harley for a moment before walking into the yard. Blake watched him stroll over to the beer trailer and pour a cup, slurp off the foam, and stand there drinking, smiling and nodding to people coming over for refills. Cat Woman had some trouble filling her cup, too much foam, and the biker showed her how to tilt the cup and do it properly. She reached out and plucked at a Sturgis pin on his leather jacket. He took out a piece of paper and showed it to her. Cat Woman looked around, met Blake's eyes, and pointed.

The biker nodded and set his beer down on a table. Picked up a cherry from the bowl and popped it into his mouth. Came back behind the lilacs. He still had the paper in his hand. It was the torn cover of Blake's *Camera and Darkroom* magazine. "Are you Blake Thorson?" he asked, looking at the mailing label.

"I am."

"My name is Mondo," the biker said. "It was my wife you were showing pornography to."

"Wait a second," Blake said. "It wasn't pornography."

"She doesn't lie."

"It was *art*. Art photos."

"Naked girls."

"A nude girl yes. From 1938. I just wanted your wife's help translating. Interpreting."

"Do you have a wife, Blake Thorson?"

"I do."

Mondo gazed at the crowd. "Is she here?"

"Yes." He pointed at Rae, up on the deck. At that moment, she was taking out one of her fake breasts and handing it to Craig Elk Nation, who hefted it and nodded approvingly.

"That figures," Mondo said.

"What's that supposed to mean?"

"Would you like some guy showing her dirty pictures?"

"No," Blake said. "I wouldn't."

He heard a squeal, laughter, and looked over the top of the lilacs. Toni was dancing with Carl under the canopy. A sloppy kind of salsa dance, with plenty of grinding. Two skinny men holding beers grabbed the ends of a table and dragged it to give them more room.

Blake moved away from the biker toward the other horseshoe pit. He reached down and swept sand back to the pile.

"How are we going to settle this?" Mondo said.

More squealing. Rae had joined Carl and Toni. The sisters were sandwiching him. Blake stood up straight. Faced Mondo and let his hand brush the revolver butt. "Why don't you just cool down, hombre?"

Mondo took off his sunglasses, tucked them into his shirt pocket.

Up on the deck, they were playing the Grateful Dead.

"Friend of the Devil," Blake said.

Mondo nodded. "Good song." He sprawled his legs.

Blake drew his revolver. His movements were slightly behind his thoughts, a result of the codeine. He cocked the Colt and sent a greasy blank down to the other horseshoe pit. Mondo had a gun, too, a small chrome automatic all but hidden in his meaty brown hand. There was a *pop* right behind Blake's *boom*. The two sounds almost merged, but Blake's was definitely first.

Blake looked down at his cowboy shirt. There was a little hole in a cactus. Right in his solar plexus, between the pearl buttons. He shoved the revolver back into his belt.

"I would have won if it was really loaded," he said.

Mondo patted at the grease splattered across his leather jacket. He shrugged and replaced the sunglasses. Spat out his cherry pit and walked back to the Harley. Drove off slowly and didn't look back.

Blake stepped through a gap in the bushes and walked to a table. He climbed up on it and stretched out. Batman came by and slapped his shoulder. "Great party, man."

"Thanks. Make sure you tell Rae."

Batman set a full beer next to Blake's ear and headed for the toilet. Blake turned the other way. Laverne and Shirley were mock kissing, doing what everybody had always speculated they did in their Milwaukee apartment after a hard day at the brewery. The men were whooping. Toni caught his eye and stuck out her tongue at him, raised her eyebrows, mouthed something he was pretty sure he'd enjoy hearing.

He touched his chest and felt the blood. The white lights strung along the fringe of the canopy blurred. The music and laughter folded into a steady drone. Blake closed his eyes. Like the beautiful girl in the Bravo photograph, he would either sleep or die. One or the other. It was no more or less complicated than that.

There Will Never Be Another Night Like This

NILS WAS RIDING IN THE trunk of a Ford LTD. He was not all that uncomfortable, in sort of a loose fetal position with his head on the spare tire. The car was a junker, and disks of light played across the trunk lid through rust holes like some kind of third-world disco strobe. The guys up front were listening to Van Halen, loud, and David Lee Roth's voice crashed around in the trunk, *I got no love, no love you'd call real.*

Nils was trying to pay attention to the car's speed, to turns, to know where he was. He had read about kidnapping victims leading police to a gang hideout. It was a matter of keeping your wits about you. You were supposed to take note of various sounds: locomotives, the whistle of a tugboat. Maybe aromas as well, the smell of a factory, the stench of a stockyard, the salty heaviness of the shore. In his case, in a moderately-sized, land-locked North Dakota college town, Nils had little to work with. He thought he detected the faint aroma of the sugar beet plant, but that could be detected everywhere in Grand Forks.

But it didn't matter. He wasn't being abducted. A little earlier, Curt and Dave had arrived at the house to pick him up. They'd been a little perturbed to learn that Nils didn't have enough money for the drive-in movie despite this being in the works for several days. "This is a pattern," Dave had said. He was Curt's older brother, a business major with a goal of becoming a millionaire by thirty. The coffee table in their apartment on Lewis Avenue was scattered with real estate books whose loud covers usually featured photos of the authors standing in front of mansions and yachts. "We always have to carry you."

"It's just a few bucks," Nils had said. "You know I'll pay you back."

"Will you, though?"

Nils had no comeback. He didn't have a very good record. He looked at Curt, more of a friend than Dave, but Curt looked down. "I mean," Dave said. "You have a job. Where does your money go?"

"Various investments."

They weren't going to abandon him; Nils knew that much. Behind their back, he called them the Flatline Brothers because they were so boring. Hanging out with Nils was the only excitement they found. Without his prompting, they might never leave the house. He had gotten them to go to an Ozzy Osbourne concert, which had been like pulling teeth, but just look, they were still talking about it almost two months later. They had a car, and Nils had energy. It was symbiosis.

They reached a compromise. Nils would ride through the admission gate in the trunk and use the cash he *did* have to help pay for the beer they were smuggling in. Dave formed a plan to pull into a parking lot not far from the drive-in to get him into the trunk unseen, but Nils said no, I'll get in *right now,* fuck you guys.

Some twisting turns, a pause at the gate, muffled voices, and then they were parking at the Starlite. The trunk opened, and Dave and Curt were peering down at him. Nils raised himself a bit and looked around. Nobody was watching, nobody cared. He climbed out and unfolded himself like a jackknife. "How was it?" Curt asked.

"I think that anytime you leave a trunk alive, you're doing pretty good." Nils opened a can of Grain Belt. Chugged it. Poked a Marlboro into his mouth. He felt like a survivor. "What's playing first again?"

"Pink Floyd, *The Wall.*"

"That's right." The lot was filling up fast. Town kids with Chevelles and Camaros and Monte Carlos had parked together like some kind of cocky armada. These were the same cars you'd see cruising Washington every weekend, pulling off now and then to collect in a parking lot before being chased away by the police. Some family station wagons and sedans and beaters like Dave's LTD were scattered around the edges. There were a few pickups owned by farm kids from beyond Grand Forks willing to drive a ways to have something to do on a Friday night. People milled around, laughing and shoving. There was an air of festivity. To the west, the sun had dropped, and the red sky was merging with the gray.

Dave was up by the hood with an aerosol can of window cleaning foam and a rag. He was working the glass pretty hard. "What the fuck are you doing?" Nils asked.

"All this dust. I want to see the movie through a clean window. Don't you?"

Nils laughed. "I guess so."

Two girls in halter tops and shorts walked by the car. They wore what looked like well-practiced, bored expressions. Nils thought of those girls in the John Updike story *A & P* which he'd read that semester in Intro to Fiction. They wedged past Dave, whose lips were pulled back in a sneer of intense concentration as he cleaned the windshield, and squeezed by Curt, who had frozen like a stunned deer in proximity to that much exposed, white flesh. Nils had never known the brothers to have girlfriends, though they liked to remark on movie stars and swivel their heads when seeing pretty girls on campus. Nils turned to watch the girls leave. Curt shook his head. "Jailbait," he said.

"Be worth the sentence," Nils said.

An hour into the movie, and Nils was already bored. He was watching from the back seat, with his chin resting on the front seat, like a little kid, or a dog. *The Wall* was okay, and Nils liked Pink Floyd, but the movie seemed to lose some of its energy in the big open space between the screen and the car, and the music wasn't served well by the dented metal speaker hanging from the window. Curt and Dave were rapt, though, oblivious to the people on their way to and from the concession stand or restrooms or just visiting other cars. Nils sipped his beer. He felt a little buzzed after a can and a half. Drinking wasn't new to him but he'd been away from it for a while. He'd spent a long time training in Tae Kwon Do, earning a brown belt, and during that time, he'd been like a Buddhist monk: rarely drinking more than a little wine and never smoking cigarettes, eating right, putting his training above everything else, practicing his forms in the morning in his college classrooms before other students arrived, letting go with jump spinning crescent kicks while walking down the street. Now that was behind him, thanks to an ill-fated romance with the Master's consort, a complicated love triangle. He had not known Kelly was the Master's consort until they started up together, and by the time she told him, it was too late, his heart was in it, and his heart had led the way, all the way down. But now he had emerged and loved his Marlboros and beer and slept well without any conflict in his heart and understood that what had happened was probably good for someone who intended to become a writer someday.

Enough was enough, and Nils told Curt and Dave he was going out for a cigarette, he'd be back. They barely acknowledged him. He pulled a fresh beer from the cooler, pushed it into his Levi's pocket, and headed for the concessions stand, a squat little concrete block building with a window to order from. It was on a slight hillside, one that called to mind a *grassy knoll*, Nils thought. There were people milling around, eating popcorn, talking, high school kids in letter jackets. They reminded him of the Socs in the movie version of *The Outsiders*, that scene at the drive-in where Ponyboy falls in love with Cherry. Nils didn't see any Greasers around, but then again, this was Grand

Forks, North Dakota, not Tulsa in the 1960s. The closest thing might have been a cluster of farm boys drinking sodas off to the side, sodas probably laced with hard liquor, talking in low tones but with their eyes darting among the girls. Kind of hungrily, Nils thought. They wore short-sleeved plaid shirts, like some kind of uniform, and new-looking blue jeans. One of them spat a load of tobacco juice at the building; it splattered into an amoeba, held for a moment, and then turned into a drip. Tacky, Nils thought. He met the eyes of the offender, a husky guy in work boots, and they held a gaze that carried something within it, a threat, a challenge. The guy started to take a step toward Nils, but the two *A & P* girls from earlier appeared and asked the little group of farmers if they had cigarettes, and this changed priorities. But the husky guy glanced back at Nils as if to say, *this isn't over*, and Nils laughed and pulled his beer from his pocket and opened it, an audacious act, out in clear view and him underage, but he didn't care. Took a long pull and stood watching the movie, listening to it on the speakers behind him on the concession stand. He adjusted his feet into a standard fighting stance, seventy percent of his weight on his back foot, thirty on the front. He felt steady, affixed to the ground but flexible. This was what being a tree would feel like, he thought.

The wind was always blowing in North Dakota, at least to some degree. Nils looked down; the stray fringes from his ripped Levi's were whipping around. His jeans were more holes than fabric, including a long tear from the knee almost up to his crotch which his sister had claimed was obscene from certain angles. He wasn't making a fashion statement. It was economics. He had one other pair of jeans, which he saved for work. He had approached his father earlier in the week, standing in front of the recliner, waiting for the old man to finish writing on one of the yellow legal pads he favored, using his briefcase as a lap desk. He was trying to get a MacArthur "genius" grant or a Guggenheim Fellowship, something like that. "Listen, man," he'd said.

"These jeans are played out. Think you can buy me some? I'll pay you back."

"Don't you have a job now?"

"I'm a college student. We're always broke."

"You don't have to pay room and board."

"This is true."

"Actually," his father had said, "ripped up Levi's are in style."

"Not anymore."

"Well, then, be a trendsetter."

So no new jeans. His mother had offered to patch them up, but Nils thought the result would be an acknowledgement that, yes, he was too poor to afford jeans. Better to just own it, like that weird guy in the neighborhood who was always touching people with his little Thalidomide flipper hand. The jeans were comfortable, and he could kick as high as his head thanks to the freedom of movement they afforded. They were just useless for work at Target or at school, where some of his professors seemed a little puritanical, wore three-piece suits every day, frowned if somebody set a can of Coke on their desk.

It was windy enough that he had trouble lighting his cigarette and stepped over to the side of the concession building for a little shelter. He had to walk by the farmers, who were with only them-selves, now that the *A & P* girls had gotten their cigarettes and paid the toll with some light flirting before heading off to weave their way among the cars again. The kind of interaction that could bring hope and frustration in all of sixty seconds. Nils leaned into the wall and created a little tipi with his hands and lighted his Marlboro. Some-thing big blocked out the light, and he turned to see the husky farmer coming over. Nils stepped away from the wall and back a step or two, giving himself room to maneuver. He wasn't sure what, if anything, was going down. The earlier glare might have meant nothing. Maybe the guy was going to ask for a light. He was a little older than Nils, early twenties, with a broad face and sort of blunt features. But it was a babyface, too, unhardened by life. Nils looked at the farmer's hands; they were oversized, but his knuckles looked unblemished. The farmer repeated his performance from earlier by spitting a load of tobacco juice against the wall. Nils wasn't sure, but thought he felt a few drops pepper his arm. "You got a problem with that?"

The Master had once said that with senior rank in Tae Kwon Do came greater responsibility; that is, your knowledge and ability gave you an edge and that the best way to emerge from a fight victorious was to avoid the fight entirely. Knowing what you could have done was enough. The Master had often unscrolled this kind of wisdom, and it was the kind of thing that Nils, in it for the entire philosophy as well as the combat secrets, liked to hear. But the Master was also known for dropping little maxims that were contradictory. *Never let anyone get away with disrespecting you.* He was half American Indian and half Italian, had spent time in Korea studying his martial art, and it seemed like his heritages and experiences sometimes collided.

Nils didn't particularly want a fight with the farmer, but there was a lot at stake, suddenly, some allegiances to consider. First and foremost, he was a townie, and this guy was from elsewhere, maybe Gilby, North Dakota, because one of his pals had a grain elevator cap from there. You certainly couldn't allow people from Gilby to move in and push their weight around. You couldn't let that kind of brazen spitting go unchecked. But mostly, Nils at that moment felt indestructible, he *owned* this little patch of ground, the Starlite Drive-In. He took a drag on his cigarette and shook his head. "You seem to be the problem child around here." Yes, it was lame, but the best he could come up with. And it was enough. He could have quoted Rilke on birds and angels, and it would have been enough. The farmer took a swing, that big fist coming around like an ugly boulder. It was as predictable as a mail train, and Nils should have been able to easily duck away from it, and maybe it was the beer, or being out of practice, and maybe it was some desire to take the first hit, to act in noble self-defense, but Nils felt the farmer's knuckles connect with his face. It was less a punch than a sort of slow grinding, plowing into his eye.

His head went back, and his vision was watery. The farmer's friends materialized nearby. Nils recovered, circled, buying a little time until his eye cleared. He shot forward, then, brought up his left knee in a high fake, and when the farmer backed up, followed through with a jump spinning right side kick into his solar plexus, one twirling movement. It was like Luke Skywalker shooting a torpedo into the Death Star's thermal exhaust port, a singular vulnerability; a big boy like that could get hammered in the face all day long and not feel it, but this was enough to stop him in his tracks. Nils had let go with a yell, a savage exhalation as he kicked, and people were looking now. He stepped back and bounced on his feet and did a little Muhammad Ali shadowboxing, ready for more. The farmer bent at the waist, holding one hand up as if to say, *what? Hold on? Give me a second?* Then he dropped to one knee. He was wheezing mightily. Nils worried for a moment that he'd kicked too hard, smashing the farmer's heart. It was possible, but he had been careful to moderate, to offer what in punching would have been more of a hard jab. Now the farmer's pals were getting agitated. He heard the words, *dirty fighting*, and he knew that, in big pockets of America, any sort of kicking was considered unsportsmanlike. Nils could see the farmer wasn't about to get up and continue anytime soon and settled his feet. A girl appeared beside Nils, standing very close, but he was reluctant to take his eyes from the farmer's friends, who seemed to be in the throes of making a decision which was going to affect him. The girl grabbed his arm and pulled him away, and then they were running, laughing.

She had a newer Chevy pickup parked at the edge of the lot, with a bench seat covered in a blue Mexican blanket. Pink Floyd was on the battered window speaker. She turned it low, had trouble with the dial, and finally knocked the speaker free and let it fall and dangle. "Fuck it," she said. She rolled up the window. "Let me take a look at that eye, Bruce Lee."

She scootched across the seat. Grabbed his chin and turned his head. "You're gonna have a great shiner tomorrow."

He shrugged.

"Does it hurt?"

"I've been hurt much worse," he said, and it was true. Early in his training, when he was a green belt, he'd been sparring with a white belt, a guy in his thirties who Nils had noticed struggled with his flexibility, had trouble kicking more than waist high--though this wasn't uncommon, it took time to stretch muscles which had never been called on to stretch. Shanlock was his name, and Nils had worked him into the corner of the dojang. This was all supposed to be light contact, it was all about technique, just practice, but Shanlock had seemed frustrated and attempted a front kick into Nils' stomach and connected squarely with his testicles. Nils would always remember the late afternoon light slanting in through the storefront windows, the dust in the air from their feet scuffing over the threadbare red carpet, the smell of sweat. *Every* man knew that quiet moment between impact and pain, it was like the calm before the storm, maybe nature set it up that way to give you a moment to prepare. In this case it passed quickly, and Nils *knew* this was going to be much worse than the other times, he knew it as soon as he looked down at Shanlock's thick leg sprouting from his groin. Shanlock apologized but without a lot of sincerity. The Master tried to help Nils, told him to stand up straight, to jump on his heels, little tricks like that. They should have used some ice but the dojang had no ice, it was rustic. The Master suggested he call it a day and, after observing Nils limping away, knowing that he walked a mile home every night, directed one of the black-belt instructors to drive him. It was Kelly, who would become his lover in the future, but back then, sex and romance were not on his mind. Ordinarily he didn't like people seeing where he lived; the house needed painting, and the yard was usually overgrown, and the picket fence surrounding the back yard needed fixing. But he directed Kelly right to the driveway, thanked her, and hobbled inside. He endured the humiliation of allowing his mother to inspect his injury, but she had no ideas for relieving the pain other than aspirin.

Nils spent a tumultuous, mostly sleepless night in an agony he might describe as pure and complete, with pain radiating from that Ground Zero into his abdomen, his thighs. The next day his scrotum was swollen so much he could not fasten his jeans, he had to wear sweat-pants. His mother took him to the clinic. He heard the resident who examined him, in the hallway, excitedly telling another resident, *it's this fucking big*. He had a scrotal hematoma, but the label didn't come with any real treatment. He refused Vicodin because he believed it would affect his training. The Master told him it was okay to skip a couple of days but stretched out on his bed, unable to walk much, in constant pain, Nils felt nothing but shame. As someone of higher rank, he should have been able to block Shanlock's kick, and he re-played the event in his mind, how he could have turned and taken the kick in his thigh, how he could have gotten his hands down there in time. It was his fault. The injury was a lesson, one that lasted a long time. It took forever to feel back to normal, and even now, two years later, he could feel ropy scar tissue in the deeper parts of his scrotum. He identified with Jake Barnes in *The Sun Also Rises*, though he could function normally in time. But the most enduring lesson was that he would likely never face the profound, variegated kind of pain he felt from the injury, and this gave him an edge in combat. So no, getting punched in the eye didn't bother him one bit.

"You brave baby," she said. He had not yet gotten a clear look at her. Now, in the muted flashing light of the movie screen, he could see she had had short blond hair, cut in the manner of a rocker, Belinda Carlisle from The Go-Go's, maybe. Perky. She was pretty in what his mother might have called an *unpretentious* way. Her name was Kat, she said, not short for anything, just Kat. She wore white shorts that made her tanned legs look all the more tan. "Hang on," she said, and left the pickup. He heard her rummaging around in the bed, and then she returned with two cans of Miller High Life. She handed one to Nils, and he held it up. Little bits of ice were running down the can, just like in a commercial. Kat moved in closer. She had an ice cube and gently pressed it to the skin around his eye, tracing the perimeter of the bruise. "It's already coming in. That boy really connected."

Nils opened his beer and took a long pull. "It happens."

She slapped his leg and leaned back. "But that *kick*. The way you just jumped up like fucking David Lee Roth and spun around and *bam*. You were just a blur."

"The goal is to end the fight without doing a lot of damage. I didn't want to really hurt the guy."

"What was it about, anyway? Did you mess with his girl? Did you fuck his girlfriend? You did, didn't you?"

Nils considered a narrative. He was a storyteller; he'd gotten into a lot of hot water in grade school spinning tales to his teachers. Then he realized, somewhat surprisingly, that the truth here was enough. "No, I don't even know the guy. He spit tobacco juice all over the building, and I kind of called him on that, you could say, and he didn't like it."

"What a slob." She popped the rest of the ice cube into her mouth and kissed him. Passed the ice cube into his mouth. They traded it back and forth until it was gone. She laughed and pulled back. Drank from her own beer and raised the can. "Here's to good manners."

"Yes," Nils said. That light action with her had fogged the windows. He felt insulated, happy in this cocoon, yet a part of him already wanted to be outside again, as if only the sky itself was an appropriate ceiling for him. The fight, brief as it was, had charged him up, and now he wished he had taken on the farmer's friends, envisioning that famous city park fight between Billy Jack and the local racists. But now she was running her finger into the rips and tears in his Levi's, so there was that, too.

"I like your truck," Nils said. "It's sharp."

"It's daddy's truck, but I drive it all the time." Her father was Duane Tandberg, she said, as if he should know the name, and he did. He saw it on yard signs all over town.

"From real estate?"

109

"One and the same." Her hand found the mother lode of rips in his jeans, the one that traversed from his inner thigh up to his crotch. She bent and ran her tongue along the pathway. Nils sipped his beer, touched the skin under his eye. It was swelling, and it was hot. His mother would be concerned, and he'd have to tell her something that satisfied her pacifist leanings, maybe say he was defending a minority who was being bullied. He jerked back, involuntarily. Kat had unbuttoned his fly, and now he was in her mouth. Just like that. It took him aback. It seemed like something that a person should be notified about. But he wasn't complaining. He closed his eyes, felt himself growing. With Kelly, this had always been a precursor to intercourse, but Kat seemed to see this act as an independent one. He reached out and slipped his hand under her shirt to cup her breast, but she pushed his hand away. Nils thought himself a generous lover—he had been trained to be and wanted to reciprocate—but settled on lightly kneading her shoulder. The pickup windows were now completely fogged, but he could hear the murmuring sound of the movie, the occasional gravel footfalls of someone walking past, someone with no idea of what was happening on the other side of the glass. Or maybe they did have an idea; sex at the drive-in was nothing new. He thought of Curt and Dave, sitting mutely in their stupid car, happy to have a spotless windshield. This kind of thing would never happen to them; they were a sort of closed circuit. It was sad, really, Nils thought. And he thought, why am I thinking about *them*? He pushed his fingers into Kat's hair, and she went faster and faster.

He didn't know how to thank her afterwards—the etiquette, what words he might use. He wondered if there was something more to come, imagined her naked on the seat, there was plenty of room. But she started to fasten his jeans again. They were button fly. "These come off easier than they go on," she said, laughing. "Maybe you better do it."

He lifted his hips and buttoned up. She leaned against him and took her beer from the dashboard. Then she reached over and started the truck, turned on the defroster, and they watched the windshield slowly clear, revealing the movie screen. They were between features now, but he didn't know what was coming up next. People were wandering around, those who'd been drinking were getting louder, some cars had left, new cars had arrived. He turned to look back toward the concession building. He didn't see the farmers. Maybe they'd gone back to Gilby, defeated in love and war. "Can I smoke in here?" Nils asked.

"I don't care."

"I wouldn't want your father to get mad at you."

"If he was, he wouldn't say anything. He's afraid to talk to me."

Nils rolled down the window a few inches, lighted a Marlboro, blew a stream of smoke through the crack. After the fight, after what Kat had just done to him, the smoke felt like some golden liquid permeating all of his cells at once. He had the sensation he was leaving his body. He wanted to say it, tell her, but didn't know how. Would he, someday? A good poet would be able to, he thought, maybe Pablo Neruda, or maybe even Charles Bukowski. He'd need a lot more experience before he could turn certain feelings and sensations into words that people would *get*.

"What do you mean, he's afraid to talk to you?"

She squeezed her breasts. "Ever since I got these, so like, four years ago."

"I've seen your father on television commercials. He seems pretty smooth. Confident."

"If I'm in a room with him, he can hardly look at me."

"Well," Nils said. When she'd gripped her own breasts, something had stirred in him, and he didn't want to talk about her father. But now that she had started talking, she wouldn't stop. She was going to UND in the fall, was he a student, he had to be, she could tell he was a thinker. She would be staying in a dorm, Selke Hall, even though her family lived not far from campus, near the golf course.

"Isn't that neighborhood surrounded by a giant fence?"

"You bet it is. It's a nice neighborhood, and we're keeping it that way."

Nils thought of his own neighborhood, in a strange pocket of town around the border marking the south and north ends of town, the usual American dividing line: there were north-end boys and south-end boys, and they had clashed for eternity. In his neighborhood were drug dealers and professors, working-class people and some old-town families who refused to move into newer homes despite being successful. A house with Victorian features and a groomed lawn might exist next to a listing house with city notices pasted to the door because the yard was an eyesore. People seemed to mind their own business. His family lived on a corner in an old farmhouse that had been carved into two apartments but now held only their family. Nils lived in the upstairs apartment kitchen, his bed wedged against a stove, his books in an ancient Kelvinator refrigerator with the door removed.

She was going to major in accounting, she said. What about him? English, he told her, and she started talking about her high school English teacher, how he wore the same sweater every day for weeks and was worse than bald, he was *mostly* bald, which just looks patchy and gross, and why couldn't she have had a teacher that looked like Nils? "The girls are going to love you," she said. He nodded, pushed his cigarette butt through the cracked window. He didn't tell her that he had no intention of teaching high school English, that he'd sooner die, that if anything, he'd be teaching at the college level and even that looked like a soul-killing proposition for a writer. With few exceptions, his professors were years away from publishing anything. Thinking about it now made him uneasy. He tried to kiss her when she was mid-sentence, and her words kept pouring into his mouth. Then she stopped and kissed him back. He could smell himself on her breath and didn't like it, but there was no way to address this, no way at all. For all he knew, she didn't like the taste of his cigarettes, so maybe they were even. He slipped his hand under her shirt and felt the absolute smoothness of her belly, warm like bread dough rising under a towel on the kitchen counter, that kind of thing. But she didn't let him near her breasts, and he didn't fight it but thought it odd that she'd go so far in one direction and not the other. Women were mysterious, and he liked it that way. Kelly had allowed and encouraged him to do anything he wanted, had instructed him in all manner of positions, configurations, sometimes adopting the same tone and mannerisms as when she was instructing at the dojang, teaching the complicated fighting patterns and forms. She'd been unabashed in her sexuality, had spoken frankly about her lush past, how she'd been with every guy on the football team in high school as a kind of personal challenge. All Nils had really wanted was to please her and went back to what he knew she liked, and he wanted it to be an expression of love, too, and not just varieties of friction. She had said she thought she could love him and that it was going to be a problem given her relationship with the Master, but in truth, he'd never *felt* her love, during sex or any other time, and wondered in hindsight if she was even capable of loving a man. Her father was a terrible alcoholic, and this seemed to enter into the mix somehow, it had to.

"Do you want another beer?" Kat asked.

"I'm good," Nils told her. He did not want to get very drunk at the drive-in, in this kind of uncontrolled environment. "In fact, I should probably be thinking about going back to where my friends are."

"Oh. You came with friends."

She sounded disappointed, but he couldn't imagine why. "They aren't good friends. They're pretty lame, actually."

"Where are they?"

Nils rolled down the window and leaned out and surveyed the array of cars. He couldn't remember where they'd parked now. Then he thought he saw the telltale squared rear end of the LTD. He tried to imagine walking back there, getting into the back seat, being shushed by Dave if he tried to tell them what had happened during the first movie, the fight, the time with Kat, a much better story than whatever was on the screen now. What *was* on the screen now? It looked like Roy Scheider flying a helicopter. Who cared? He knew this much: he could not be contained like that, waiting for the movie to be over, trapped in that ugly car. "I'm not seeing them. They might have left already."

Kat slid over to get behind the wheel. "Let's get out of here, then." She deftly maneuvered the truck forward into the wider lane, and they moved toward the exit. He turned his head so that Dave and Curt wouldn't see him leaving, but then he remembered the little interaction regarding his finances, how insulting that was, how he'd had to travel in the trunk, and thought, fuck them, anyway, even though he knew they had a point, he *was* usually broke, enjoying their beer, a charitable hamburger now and then. His job at Target was part time, and when he cashed his check, the money just evaporated. People his age had checkbooks and car loans. How did that happen? He didn't have rent or bills except for student loans he wasn't going to have to start paying on for years. His father had warned him against working too many hours while in school. He'd seen it a million times, he said, good students who started putting in more and more hours and their schoolwork suffered. This after Nils had said he wanted to rent an apartment, when he thought he had a future with Kelly, which he thought because one afternoon, at her parents' house, the site of all their indiscretions, they'd shared a frozen Schwan's pizza at the table like a real couple, and she'd said, "I think living with you would be a blast." Nils had brought that up when she was breaking up with him, and she claimed no recollection, and furthermore told Nils he would be learning soon enough that people said all kinds of things when they were *fucking*—the brain chemicals were like a downed power line, arcing and sparking and smoking hot. "You'll get over it," she'd said, and it may have been the most truthful thing she ever told him. Now he felt lucky to have emerged from the love triangle, though it ended his training, because he was no longer welcome at the dojang.

In reality, he missed the training more than the girl. He had seen the Master only once since then, at the mall, when he and Danny Cook were out looking for loose Target carts. The Master was walking into J.C. Penney's with his girlfriend by his side, and Kelly walking a few feet behind them, head slightly bowed. Much of his bitterness had been replaced by something like pity. She was in a far stranger and more difficult place than he had been in.

Instead of turning left on Highway 81, the way back to town, Kat turned right. Nils said nothing. He wasn't in a hurry to get home; it was barely eleven. She could drive all the way to Fargo for all he cared. He was still adjusting to having his evenings free. His training at the dojang had been five nights a week, an hour helping instruct the beginner class, showing people—some much older than him—how to properly make a fist, how to lift their leg and pivot and thrust for a side kick. They were always frustrated with how their bodies resisted these new ways of moving, and Nils always reassured them, in no time at all this would be second nature, and it was true for those who stuck it out. Then an hour in the advanced class: learning, practicing, sparring. There were moments when it felt almost holy to be there. Nobody ever understood what he meant by that. But there was a quiet that would fall over the dojang, a respect, a history, that was palpable, and that was his favorite thing. One night, Kelly, in the middle of an intense sparring match, began to menstruate, her white cotton *dobok* pants streaking with blood. She hadn't noticed, that's how focused she'd been. The Master didn't stop the match, and nobody watching said a thing, didn't smirk or even glance at each other. Nils had just started college, analyzing literature for the first time, learning about symbolism, and it had struck him that he was witnessing some kind of metaphor, a rich one, but could only file it away because he had no way to work with it.

"I'm not sure if I'll be pledging a sorority or not," Kat said, as if they'd been discussing this already. "My parents think I should, you know, for the connections. Because, like, I'm not exactly going to an ivy league school, so I need to take advantage of whatever I can."

Nils felt a little irritated. He wasn't entirely sure why. "I guess it depends on what you want to do with your life."

"What do you mean?"

"If you want to hang out with Greek life assholes in the future, it's probably a good idea to start right now."

He thought she might be offended but she only laughed. "You're such a hoot. You're such a rebel."

She turned off the highway and headed down a gravel road, stopped the truck and climbed out. "Have to pee," she said, giggling. She moved off into the darkness. Nils took the opportunity to do the same. He looked up at the sky. Away from ambient light, the stars were bold and seemed to pulsate, throbbing a silent backbeat to the night, something he believed that only he could detect, as if the universe existed in service to him alone tonight. He felt *that* good. When Kat returned, they opened fresh beers, and she popped the tailgate, and they sat in the sweet wind with its faint aroma from the freshly laid crops. He didn't know what was growing in the fields surrounding them; it could have been sugar beets, could have been soybeans.

"My dad bought up a bunch of this land around here."

"Is he a farmer, too, along with the real estate?"

"No. But he says town is growing south and someday that land is going to be very valuable. He'll sell it off one chunk at a time. It's a long-term thing. A long-term investment. In the meantime, he leases it to farmers."

"That's clever."

"There's like, tax benefits involved. I don't understand it all. But I'll have to, because I'm an only child."

Nils waved his hand. "Someday all of this will be yours."

He was being a little facetious, but she nodded kind of gravely. "I really wish I had a brother or sister."

There was a hint of vulnerability in her voice, and he found himself attracted to her. To that? The vulnerability itself? He finished his beer and threw the can into the ditch. She did the same, and they returned to the cab, but after she turned on the ignition, he took her hand and pulled her close. They kissed for a while. When "True" by Spandau Ballet came on the radio, he unbuttoned her shorts and pulled them down. He wanted to consume her, he felt that hunger. He closed his mouth around her navel, and she gasped, and he took this as consent to go further and he did, flinging her shorts and panties away and lifting her to his face with both hands under her rear end, like a chalice. She gripped his hair and pulled it hard. She was only his second woman, and he was struck by how she tasted like Kelly but not like her at the same time. Kelly had enjoyed this a lot, had said he'd never be lonely as long as he did this, took his time. He had liked pleasing her, he had wanted to make her love him, to give her more and more reasons to stay with him, to stack those reasons up against the stack the Master had built. It hadn't been enough. Now Kat started to quiver and moan, and she bucked so hard her hipbone drove into his black eye, and he felt pain radiating across his face, but it was a good pain, it seemed to fit with the overall experience. They lay sort of glued to each other for a while, listening to the radio. Then she dressed herself and fixed her hair and used both hands to sort of fix his hair as well, licking her fingers before patting at the sides of his head. "Mister, where in the world did you learn how to do *that?*"

"I guess it just comes naturally."

"Well." She put the pickup in gear and drove on, to the next intersection, and turned around with a flourish, spraying gravel in a wide arc behind the spinning tires. He wanted to believe they were even now, that some business deal had been concluded with both of them satisfied, ready to shut their briefcases and walk away in different directions. But she seemed energized, ebullient, like they were at the beginning of something. Together. "I can't wait to show you off to my friends."

The idea startled him. "I should probably be getting on home pretty soon."

She gave him a theatrical pout. "Why?"

No good lie came to him. He was eighteen, he could do whatever he wanted, join the Marines, vote. When he was seeing Kelly, he regularly didn't get picked up by her until very late, and after their time together, he would refuse her offer of a ride home, *chivalry*, and walk twenty blocks back to his neighborhood. He welcomed that time to decompress, to replay their encounter, to search for signs he was winning her heart. His father knew of his odd hours and, out of either respect or reluctance, never really asked about it. Theirs was not a family known for sharing personal information.

"I might be a little tired," he said now.

"You didn't seem tired five minutes ago." They reached the highway, turned right, floated past the Starlite where the movie was still on the screen, the faces huge and frightening seen from the road. Highway 81 soon became Washington Street, the main drag, and it was alive with cruisers burning gasoline, going up and down, up and down. Kat swiveled her head as she drove, until she seemed to find what she was looking for, and whipped into a drug store parking lot where a few people stood around talking. Nils had never been a part of this scene; without that essential ingredient, a car, he was hobbled. The few friends he had now were older, not interested in aimless driving. Dave and Curt were gas misers, and their car would have been laughed at, anyway. Kat parked and climbed out, and Nils felt he had to do the same. There were several boys and girls chattering, the boys with puffed out chests and the girls with their hands on cocked hips. Nils knew none of them and felt an instant awkwardness. Tae Kwon Do had been his social life for a long time. Once in a while someone had a gathering, a backyard barbeque or a party, and they often invited Nils, and they treated him like an adult and not a teenager, offering him wine, listening to his opinions when they talked about Ronald Reagan or whatever. The Master and his girlfriend and Kelly rarely came to these events, and people acted differently when they weren't around, drinking a little more, laughing a little more loudly, like kids whose parents were gone for the night. Nils was known for being somber in the dojang, and when he relaxed and got a little loose from wine, people were always surprised and seemed to like it. Now and then, someone would remark on the Master, try to inject a little speculation and gossip, but this never went very far for some reason, as if they were scared he had eyes and ears everywhere.

Now Kat grabbed his hand and pulled him into the mix. "This is Nils."

"What happened to his *face?*" a girl asked.

"He got into a fight at the Starlite. He kicked this guy's *ass.*"

The boys nearby scrutinized Nils silently, sizing him up. Nils nodded.

Kat pulled one of her friends aside, buried her face in her friend's huge teased-out hair, said something. Her friend's eyes widened, and she stared at Nils and started laughing. He shrugged and smiled. He thought, *I have nothing in common with any of these people.* But he didn't really want to go home, either. His father would be in bed now, on his strange sleep schedule that had him up at two in the morning to sit in his chair and read and write and watch CNN. His mother would still be up, enjoying the quiet, the solitude, working on her jigsaw puzzle of the Norwegian fjords and smoking one True Green after another. Nils imagined his little brother was out here on Washington with his friends, if they were able to get one of their beat-up cars running. His sister lived with her son in an apartment near the family house. She was probably entertaining Muslim students, sitting around on a Persian rug talking about Rumi, her favorite poet, serving tea. No, Nils didn't want to go home yet, but he didn't want to be here. He lighted a cigarette and faced the street, feigning interest in the convoy of cars. He could not talk about four-barrel carburetors or gear ratios: it wasn't part of his *lexicon;* he could appreciate these older muscle cars aesthetically, but that was about it. Kelly owned a red Mustang, and she had let him drive it once, laughing at how he hugged the shoulder and stayed below the speed limit. This had been one afternoon when the Master sent her to Crookston to fill in for a teacher who was gone, at a small dojang the Master had some affiliation with. He had asked Nils to go along as her assistant. They were involved then, and it was like a great gift, time together in broad daylight with no fear of discovery. They'd taught the class, and after, went to Dairy Queen for ice cream and sat at a picnic table in the shade like a real couple. Kelly had worn a sort of body-hugging summer dress, sleeveless, revealing her tanned and toned arms, and Nils had been aware of and pleased by the attention she had drawn from the men in this farm town, the doubletakes and sidelong glances. This was the day when she had snatched his hand up in hers and stared at him hard across the splintery picnic table and said, "More than one thing can be true at the same time. Remember that." He'd looked at her wheat-colored hands, her slender fingers. Her hands were smooth except for her knuckles, toughened from thousands of pushups on the hard carpeted floor. Nils himself had calloused knuckles; he'd taken to punching hard surfaces, trees and houses and even concrete, not hard enough to break his bones but hard enough to turn his hands into better weapons. It was part of his philosophy that a warrior should always be training, not just for whatever hours a martial arts class was being held. "Is that from Heinlein?" he'd asked, because she was a Heinlein fan, encouraged him to read *Stranger in a Strange Land*. She had laughed. "No, it's from life."

Kat came over and stood square against him and put her arms around his neck. "Kiss me," she said. Nils balked. There was something contrived about this; he'd only known her for a few hours. It was kid stuff. Nils was glad he had not gone to high school. His family had lived on the Navajo Reservation for several years, and he'd been homeschooled and then started college early when they landed in Grand Forks. He'd missed out on what seemed like a lot of nonsense, though he sometimes wondered about the good things he might have missed out on. He thought he might have liked shop class or working on a school newspaper. He would have probably had some girlfriends already before Kelly, and so it might not have affected him so profoundly when she broke up with him. But *this* he could live without. Kat was looking up at him expectedly. He kissed her, a peck, and patted her back. The others watched and then turned away. They were talking about a keg party somewhere by the river north of town. Kat joined in. He thought her voice was changing, becoming sort of high and excited to match the voices around her. She motioned him to the pickup, and they climbed back into it. "Do you want to drive?"

"That's okay."

"Cause some guys don't like riding bitch."

Nils had never heard it referred to that way. "I guess some guys aren't very confident in their masculinity."

"Sassy," she said. She nodded at the others, who were getting into their cars. "I had to give them a hard time. They were supposed to be at the Starlite."

"What do you mean?"

"We were all gonna meet up at the movie, but I'm the only one who showed up. I was looking for them when I saw you fighting that guy."

"Ah," Nils said.

"I guess our wires got crossed."

"They weren't pranking you?"

"What? No. They're my buds. No."

But she bit her lip now and went silent. They pulled onto Washington and headed north. "They wouldn't do that," she said.

"I'm sure plans are all over the place on a Friday night. This early in the summer. Everyone's trying to do everything all at once."

She said nothing. At a stop light some kids in a rasping convertible pulled up alongside them. The driver looked to be about fourteen, with a blond mullet and a dangly earring. He gunned the engine and leveled a stare at Kat. To Nils it looked like the kid was joking around, trying to flex his rusty jalopy against Kat's nearly brand-new pickup, but she revved the engine, that big V8 making the seat tremble. He was relieved she was feeling playful again, but then the light changed and the truck lurched ahead, easily left the convertible behind because they *weren't trying to race after all*, and sloped down through the underpass beneath the railroad tracks. Kat was gripping the steering wheel with both hands; they were going fast. They went into the other lane, she tried to correct, and then the pickup was starting to roll. Things really did switch to slow-motion, his stomach rose, and he was reaching for something to hang on to; she at least had the steering wheel as an anchor, but he had nothing; he heard the sound of scraping metal, crunching, caught a glimpse of a shower of sparks over the road. He saw the unfastened seatbelt flapping like a flag, useless, taunting him, and then he was simply floating, and he thought he might be heading into the spirit world, hurtling through time and space, because when he opened his eyes he was looking into light, a bright haloed light, and wasn't that how they usually described it?

He watched them extricate Kat from the pickup while a paramedic checked him over. Nils had imagined she was dead from the way the cab was nearly flattened, from the scene itself, glass everywhere, bits and pieces of mirror and chrome littering the street. They didn't have to use the famous jaws of life to free her, but it took several firefighters to get her out. Nils couldn't really see what they were doing from his vantage point, but he was surprised when they loaded her onto a stretcher and didn't pull the sheet over her face like in the movies and even more surprised when he heard her laugh. She saw Nils watching and blew him a kiss. Then they slid her into the ambulance and took her away.

The paramedic played a flashlight all over Nils, peppering him with questions. He thought Nils should go to the hospital to be evaluated but he couldn't make him, he said. He prodded at the inflamed skin around his eye, but Nils didn't mention that it was from earlier.

Nils thought it must have seemed odd that he barely had a scratch. He had found himself on a strip of grass looking up at a streetlight in a sort of reverie that only broke when the flashing lights and sirens intruded.

Now Nils was approached by a cop who was spending a lot of time fiddling with a notebook. What was the driver's name? She was a Tandberg, he said. Kat. The cop raised his eyebrows. "Her father is the real estate guy," Nils said.

"What is your relationship to the driver? Boyfriend?"

"More of an acquaintance. I met her at the Starlite, and she was giving me a ride home. I barely know her."

"Do you know how this happened?

"No," Nils said. "I mean, it happened so fast. Nothing out of the ordinary was going on."

The cop stared at him for a long time. "Normally, something has to happen to cause an accident. People are arguing, they're going too fast for the conditions, they're screwing around."

Nils feigned great, concerned reflection. "Well, the only thing I can think of is that she was very excited about being invited to a party, and she was talking a lot, you know."

"Distracted."

"I'd say so."

"Girls, right?

"Yes."

The cop laughed. He had all he needed. But he waved toward Kat's red cooler, on its side and open, a little ice and several cans of beer surrounding it. "You might want to collect your beer, son. We wouldn't want someone to think Miss Tandberg was drinking when this happened."

Nils gave him a blank look.

The cop sighed. "Her *father* will have enough to worry about, won't he?"

"Of course," Nils said. He understood. He picked up the loose cans, shoved them into the cooler. The bent lid would not shut all the way. He started walking back down Washington. The paramedic had told him he might have injuries, especially back injuries, that would not surface right away, that he could wake up in agony tomorrow morning, or go to lift something in a few days and be wracked with pain. That kind of thing. He had no recollection of landing after being thrown from the pickup. He wondered how things would have gone if the window had not been rolled down all the way.

Home was only a few blocks away, but instead of turning left at the intersection of Demers and Washington, he kept going, passing the red cooler from left hand to right, right to left. He thought the word *albatross*. Like it was going to be a memento of the accident, of Kat, that he would be carrying forever. He reminded himself that he had nothing to feel guilty about. He hadn't been driving and didn't have a chance to intervene. What she'd done, she'd done so suddenly, turning the pickup into an expression of her emotion. He wondered if he should check in on her at the hospital but imagined her parents there, wondering who he was, finding a way to blame him for what happened. No thanks. He drifted away from the sidewalk to cut through parking lots and avoid being so close to the cars on Washington. Any pedestrian was a target for carloads of kids. He'd once had a full cup of soda thrown at his chest when walking at night. He'd been outraged. It was a completely unprovoked attack, and he'd tried to chase down the car on foot, ready to kick the snot out of everyone in it.

Now he heard his name called. He turned in a circle, saw his little brother standing with a few of his friends in the La Campana parking lot. They looked very young, like the Little Rascals, but one of them had a driver's license and a borrowed station wagon. They were listening to Def Leppard on a boom box on the hood and smoking cigarettes cupped in their hands like tough guys. "Shouldn't you be home?" Nils said.

His brother spat. "Do you really care?"

"No."

"What happened to your eye?"

His brother's friends ebbed closer. A black eye was something to celebrate. "Long story," Nils said.

"Did you win? Did you kick his ass?"

"Let's just say he started it, and I finished it."

"He's a brown belt in Korean karate," his brother said. "Don't fuck with him. What's in the cooler?"

Nils lifted the lid to reveal a half-dozen beers.

"Oh man, give us those."

"Are you crazy?"

"Come on. That's not enough for us to get drunk on."

Nils considered the logic. They'd each have a beer and a half, something to make the night more magical. He was tired of carrying it around, anyway. He set the cooler down. "Ten bucks."

"No fucking way."

He picked the cooler up and started to walk. The boys pooled their money, handed over rumpled bills. "Good enough," Nils said. He kept walking.

He stopped at the Valley Dairy store and bought a fresh pack of Marlboros and packed them against the heel of his hand as he walked. He ducked into the Crestwood Restaurant, an all-night pancake house. A long row of booths ran parallel to the street, under windows that stretched the length of the building. Nils went to the last one and sat down. He had been to the Crestwood a few times before with Curt to study, because the coffee was a bottomless pot and you could sit for a long time. But Curt preferred the campus library because it was quiet and free and didn't understand why Nils liked the restaurant, the motion and sound, the endless opportunities to study people in action, to imagine what their stories were. Curt was an English major but not really a writer and didn't seem very curious about things.

The waitress was a dark-haired woman, mid-twenties or even older. Nils noted the lines radiating from the corners of her eyes, the sort of hardness of her mouth. No doubt she lived a tough life, he thought, maybe the opposite of Kat's life. Like everyone else, she seemed to notice his black eye. But she didn't pry, and he liked that, liked that she understood that he might not want to talk about it. "You look like you've had some night," was all she said.

"So far," Nils said. She laughed as she walked away. He lighted a cigarette and rested his elbows on the table and smoked. He glimpsed his reflection in the window. He looked like any guy smoking a cigarette in a twenty-four hour restaurant, nothing special. Nobody would guess that he had just walked away from a serious accident. He spooned some ice into his coffee. Or that he had been training for so long and so intently at a dojang, that his training had become an essential part of his life.

After the break-up, Nils had signed up for the only other Tae Kwon Do class in town, lessons through the YMCA. His first night there he'd realized just how good he'd had it. The teacher was a sec-ond-degree black belt with a beard and paunch. Everyone called him Bill, not *master*, not the Korean *sabumnim*. And he seemed a little put off by the respect Nils demonstrated. The class was a mishmash of age and ability. Nils had thought his brown belt might make him a resource, that he could add something to the class, but Bill told him that, because he was trained under World Tae Kwon Do Federation standards, they would have to take a "wait and see" approach to how his rank would be recognized. They did not bow to the American and Korean flags. It was like having been in the Marines and suddenly finding yourself in the Cub Scouts. They did not have a dedicated room at the YMCA, just a corner of a room, and they had to contend with people going from the stairs to the gym, people dribbling basket-balls and talking and laughing. Nils had tried to stick it out, but on his last night he was horrified when, in the locker room, Bill untied his black belt and tossed it to the floor. The dirty floor. "See you

Monday?" he asked, and Nils said yes, of course, knowing he would not.

He had walked home, underneath the Demers overpass, and as he crossed the railroad tracks, when he was in the deep, impenetrable shadows, started to cry. He cried for a long time, and there were different tracks to his crying, like on a record album: violent frustration, deep sorrow, wide-open grief. Then he slapped himself on the face very hard, both sides, and said, *fuck it,* and went home. Sat at the kitchen table and watched his mother working on an astrology chart through a huge, Sherlock Holmes-style magnifying glass. She ran a modest mail-order business doing the charts for people. It was time-consuming and involved studying old books filled with tables and diagrams and then interpreting how someone's time and place of birth affected their lives, their hopes, their problems. Nils had once quietly done the math and calculated that she was earning far less than minimum wage, but it was a labor of love. Normally, when someone she knew entered into a romance, his mother offered to do a couple's chart. But when he began seeing Kelly, even when it was apparent that he was seeing her almost every day, she had not offered, as if she knew there was something already doomed about it. And when everything fell apart, she didn't really seem surprised. He had very reluctantly let on that it was a love triangle involving the Master, but only to explain why he was no longer training, and that was enough. That night at the table after returning from the YMCA, she probably could tell that he had been crying but said nothing and likewise said nothing when he tapped one of her menthols from the package and lighted it, sucked in the smoke, the first time he'd smoked in a couple years. He'd grown lightheaded, his capillaries had numbed, and it was just what he needed.

He sipped his coffee and stared into the middle distance. It was well after midnight, and people were starting to show up after being at the bars, a little boisterous, ordering big breakfasts, still using the loud voices they'd been using in the loud bars. Nils felt a little awkward being alone in a booth without someone to talk to, something to do, a book or a notebook. Every action, tapping the ash from his cigarette, taking a sip of coffee, seemed exaggerated, like he was on stage in a play, about to turn to the audience and start a monologue.

A young couple nearby was sitting on the same side of a booth, sharing a piece of blueberry pie. They looked a little unkempt, hair mussed, and the woman's makeup was smeared. The man ran his finger through the pie and brought it up to the woman's mouth, and she closed her lips around it and shut her eyes in exaggerated ecstasy. Nils looked away, did not want to be caught looking at this. He wished they'd sat on the other side of the booth so that he could only see the backs of their heads. They were acting a little extreme, but at the same time, he was jealous of them, of that totally unabashed affection in public. Except for their trip to Crookston, he and Kelly had never had a public date. When the county fair was on, Nils had gone with his brother, just to walk around. This was toward the end of things with Kelly, when Nils was sort of nearing peak frustration, finding it harder and harder to be two people at once, the loyal student, and the secret boyfriend. Perhaps because of this, at the fair, he'd been acutely aware of the throngs of couples, people holding hands; even when he looked up, he could not escape it, because they were on the Ferris wheel, too, embracing, making out. He had won a stuffed rabbit at the shooting gallery and thought about saving it for Kelly, but the idea just seemed dumb, and he handed it to a little girl who was having some kind of temper tantrum. She threw it to the ground, embarrassing her mother.

But he *had* gone on a date recently. A sort-of date. Her name was Tracy, and she was one of the cashiers at Target. Upstairs in the break room, she'd approached Nils and said she remembered him from taking Tae Kwon Do classes with her little brother. Nils drew a blank at first. Many people signed up, went for a while, dropped out. It wasn't for everyone, and it wasn't like what they might have seen in the movies. The first half of every class was devoted to conditioning,

tons of push-ups and sit-ups, leg lifts, kicking in place, lots of stretch-
ing. Some people didn't like that, they wanted to learn techniques the
whole time, but the principle was sound: you needed a strong back,
a strong core, flexibility. While he was talking to Tracy, he tried to
remember her, and then it clicked: she and her brother, nice kids, shy,
they liked to be partners. They'd come for a few sessions and then
didn't come anymore. "I wondered where you guys went," Nils said. He
noticed that she blushed a little. She and her brother weren't comfortable with the bowing and with calling a teacher *master*. "It felt a little
like paganism," she said. "Our dad told us to stop going." Nils allowed
that he could understand that. He didn't go anymore himself, he said,
but didn't elaborate. A few days later, he was going from lane to lane
collecting clothes hangers from the bins—it was a Saturday and the
bins filled up fast—and Tracy said, "There's a movie I'd like to take
you to." Was she asking him out on a date? It seemed so, but she was
awfully matter of fact about it, with none of the windup he would
have expected, not even a fluttering eyelash, like in the movies. Sure,
he told her, he'd like that. She knew he didn't own a car and offered to
pick him up. He wrote his address on a piece of register tape.

The night of the movie, he took some time getting ready. It felt
good to be openly preparing for a date. He endured some teasing from
the family. His mother was interested in who this Tracy person was.
Did he know her birthday and year? No, mother, he didn't. He would
try to find out. He didn't tell her that if Tracy thought Tae Kwon Do
was paganism, she probably wouldn't be that keen on astrology. His
own family was mainly Catholic, depending on how his father felt
about the Vatican at any given moment. His mother was a Lutheran
minister's daughter but not a churchgoer. She liked her cigs and the
occasional Jim Beam.

He wore his work jeans and a sort of western-style shirt with
pearl snaps. He didn't like it very much, but his wardrobe was woe-
fully thin. With Kelly, seeing her on the sly late at night, he had worn
mainly track clothes and running shoes, whatever t-shirt happened

to be clean at the moment, clothing meant for those long walks home alone. You look nice, his mother had said, slipping him a ten-dollar bill, as if he was in junior high and not someone who a few months earlier had been sleeping with an older woman several nights a week, always fearful of being caught, his brain scrambled most of the time. It had struck him that his antics might have affected his parents more than he ever would have thought, given them cause to worry.

Tracy had picked him up in her father's work van, with a steam cleaning unit mounted inside and a smiling carpet painted on the side. She looked nice, hair made up, in a sort of billowy blouse, a skirt that was longer than he might have preferred, like the skirts worn by waitresses at Village Inn, but he enjoyed seeing her shiny knees for a moment. He felt comfortable with her, but he was on guard, too, presenting his best self. He did not smoke a cigarette. They talked about work, some of the people, their manager, but she didn't know much gossip. She was in her first year at UND for elementary education. At the theater, she insisted on paying—she'd asked *him*, after all—but allowed him to buy popcorn. They were there to see something called *The Prodigal*, which he'd never heard of. He'd looked over at Tracy; her face was smooth and shiny in the dim light, with a glow that seemed to come from within her, like some sort of ocean phosphorus. She reached down and tugged at her skirt but not in the direction he would have hoped. He imagined that putting his arm around her might be a little too much. The movie moved slowly, involved a guy who didn't like his Christian family, left home, did some bad things, and eventually returned not only to his family but to God. There was a message here, not a subtle one; it was being clubbed into the audience like callous hunters bashing baby seals. More than a few people had exclaimed at the ending and applauded. Out in the parking lot, Tracy wanted pretty badly to know what he thought. "I like happy endings," he told her, and this seemed to satisfy her. There was no goodnight kiss or mention of further dates, so he was at a loss to understand if she was interested in him at all, if this outing had any meaning. His family wanted to know how it went. He told them about the movie. His father laughed. "That wasn't a date. You were evangelized."

They'd hung out a little at work, but it was mostly small talk. Now it occurred to him that maybe she was just terribly shy, waiting for him to make a move. It was his turn to ask, after all. Wasn't it? Maybe she was old-fashioned. Those long skirts spoke to a time when men did the courting or whatever. He had no experience in normal dating. Kat had lured him into her pickup before she even knew his name. And he had gotten Kelly into his life, he believed, by being in her proximity and just staring at her until she understood his intentions, trying to *will* her to become receptive until finally, giving him a ride home after a tournament, she'd told him that she knew he liked her, and yes, they could get something going, but also told him about her entanglement with the Master. He had really only heard the word *yes*, deciding that if he only had a chance, things would fall into place eventually, and she would be his and his alone. She had said something else later that night. "You can never *ever* tell me you love me." It had seemed odd and awfully melodramatic. But he was alone with a girl he had been coveting, thinking she was beyond reach. His dreams were coming true. He would have agreed to anything.

He took a sip of coffee too quickly and choked, coughed, kept coughing. He felt his face turning red, more from the idea of people staring at him than anything else. Something popped from his throat and landed on the table and skidded a few inches. When he recovered and felt like nobody was watching, he picked it up. It was a little square chunk of automotive glass. He rubbed it clean and turned it in his hands; it caught the light like some kind of jewel. He imagined having it set into a ring, showing people. *This was in my lungs after I was in a pickup that flipped over.* He pressed his fingers to his chest and wondered if there was more in there. Took a deep breath but didn't feel anything unusual.

He wasn't tired, but he felt like he'd been in the restaurant long enough, smoking too many cigarettes. And drinking too much coffee; he felt wired. Most of the bar rush people were leaving, and the waitresses were busy clearing the mess. He laid a five-dollar bill on the table and left. Walked through the same quiet neighborhoods he had walked through so many times before, after leaving Kelly's. The streets were usually deserted, the houses dark, and he had sometimes felt like a jungle animal—a panther, perhaps—moving through a sleeping village. Once, some cops had pulled up and called him over to their car, wanting to know what he was doing out there in the middle of the night. Insinuating he was some sort of burglar. He'd been in a particularly foul mood as he often was after being with Kelly, when his feelings were intense and he was frustrated by the nature of their affair. So he'd been short with the cops, asking what law he was breaking by walking around in a city in the United States of America. He wasn't about to say he was on his way home after being with his girlfriend because that could lead to being asked who his girlfriend was, and he was imaginative enough to foresee her somehow being questioned and this leading to all kinds of problems. He was upset, standing by the squad car, and began to wish for an altercation, a fight. He had known he would lose that fight, but even this was appealing—even being beaten up a little, clubbed on the head, would help level out the pain he was feeling on the inside. But the cops did the worst thing possible, just laughed, and one of them said, "No problem, brother," and they drove off.

He reached his house and sat on the weathered gray wooden steps facing Oak Street. This had been his spot for the longest time when he was involved with Kelly. He'd never known on a given night if he'd be seeing her. They didn't plan anything. He knew she was at the Master's place often and that she sometimes spent the night. The Master's girlfriend knew about it, and when Kelly had started to explain the dynamics of their situation, Nils had held up his hand, saying stop, he didn't want to know, he didn't want to have to consider *that* on top of everything else. He liked the Master's girlfriend, she was a good teacher, an accomplished competitor, very kind. By then, he was already compartmentalizing, that was the word for it, he was able to go to practice and respect the Master, look up to him, remain loyal on every front but one.

He would sit on the steps late at night, listening to the radio, waiting without expectation. Sometimes he would practice his forms on the lawn, over and over, until the dewy grass bore a capital letter "I" pattern from his movements. And sometimes, the glass storm door on the house across the street would light up from a car coming up Fifth Avenue. It got so that he could tell by the way the storm door glowed if it was Kelly's Mustang. He'd go to the car, and they'd drive to her house and go down to the basement and sit on the couch and talk. He liked talking to her; she was well-read, about to start a graduate degree in psychology. She was interested in his writing and liked the few short pieces he'd read to her, laughing when he hoped she would. They talked about people in the dojang but never about the Master. But the time on the couch never lasted as long as he would have liked, and soon enough they were off to the guest room with its small window near the ceiling, and its dark wood paneling, and the closet that smelled of mothballs. Sometimes she played Rod Stewart on a cassette, but quietly because her parents were asleep upstairs. After, she'd perform private, mysterious rituals in the bathroom while he got dressed. This was their usual date, and it hardly varied, though if her parents were out of town, they might use her bedroom upstairs, allowing him a glimpse into her life through the books on the shelf, the Tae Kwon Do medals and trophies on the wall, the big Al-Anon poster with the Serenity Prayer on the back of the door.

He lighted a cigarette. It felt strange to be on the steps now. Nobody was coming for him. And yes, after she broke up with him, he had maintained a nightly vigil on the steps, every song on the radio now a melancholy ballad about his heartbreak. He had done this for a week or so, believing that she would arrive, her mind changed. His sorrow had turned to anger, and then to confusion, and a big question: how were they able to see each other so often with the Master unaware? The Master was highly observant, could appear to not be paying attention, talking to someone by the door, and then walk over and point out that you had too much weight on your left leg, and he would be right. It didn't really add up, but the possibilities were like some new territory he did not want to be alone in, the mysterious Congo in Joseph Conrad's *Heart of Darkness*, another Intro to Fiction reading assignment.

Now he prodded the skin under his eye until the pain overwhelmed the thoughts he did not want to be thinking. But he sure wished Kelly could have seen him in action tonight. The fight, Kat, everything. He was a different person than the one she'd seen last, blubbering like a baby in her car after he had told her he could not handle it any longer, that she had to make a choice. He was a different *man*. He wished the Master could have seen him tonight. He wished they *all* could have seen him.

Lightning flashed to the west, and the thunder wasn't very far behind. The air was cooling. The two great evergreens flanking the yard began to sway. Nils rubbed his bare arms. He wanted to go inside for something to drink, and he was a little hungry, but the blue glow in the living room window meant his father was up. He'd see the black eye and accept whatever story Nils told him and then no doubt launch into his own story about a black eye he got in the 1950s in Tacoma when he and some of his IWW buddies got into a barfight with some Communists over ideology and a beautiful, raven-haired waitress or maybe it was an aging prostitute with a heart of gold cradled his head against her ample bosoms and tended to his wounds, that sort of thing, a story he would no doubt have heard before. Would he do the same thing to his own children someday? Would they roll their eyes and say, *we've heard about the drive-in fight a million times already*?

He dug in his pocket for the little piece of window glass and rolled it between his thumb and forefinger. He remembered the screeching sound of steel against asphalt, how gravity had been suspended within the cab of the pickup, like those films of astronauts in space, a tube of toothpaste floating in midair. He had not been scared in those chaotic moments, though things had happened too quickly to be scared. But he had not been scared right after, either. Stretched out on the grass, listening to the sirens getting louder, the event had seemed to be just one more scene in a story in which he was the hero, a story that could not go on without his presence.

More lightning. The storm was coming in quickly, but he remained on the steps. It wasn't raining yet. It seemed improbable that, just a few hours earlier, he'd been standing in the yard with Curt and Dave having a banal conversation about money, with no idea what lay ahead. He didn't think he would tell them about what happened. They wouldn't believe it, anyway; they'd think it was a story to explain why he had ditched them. They might believe the fight since he had the black eye, but not fooling around with a girl in a pickup and not the wreck on top of that. It wasn't plausible. It was like that story about Hemingway getting into two plane crashes in forty-eight hours, but you could believe *that* because it absolutely seemed like something that would happen to Hemingway.

He thought of Tracy, who would never fit into a Hemingway story, unless maybe as a wartime nurse. She had a life plan, she had told him. They'd gone on break together and walked through the mall to the Orange Julius for a drink and sat and watched people moving by, some of them pushing Target carts. Target was affixed to the mall and didn't mind people taking carts from the store and using them while shopping elsewhere. Nils thought they believed it was good advertising somehow, those red carts all over the place. But it also meant that people left the carts in every parking lot around the mall so that once every shift, Nils and his crew had to walk around the perimeter gathering them up. Sometimes they made a train so long they had to take turns pushing. Once, there were so many carts, Danny Cook said *fuck it* and jogged back to Target to get his car, his big Mercury, and pushed the train with his bumper while Nils steered. They drew a few looks. It was probably a company violation of some kind, so they had parked the car and gone back to manual pushing just before reaching the store. It was the hardest part of the job, but it was also their favorite part of the job, because it allowed them to be away from the store, from the managers and especially the customers.

Tracy had said, "I have a plan, though you better believe it when I say God might have other plans. It's like what proverbs says. 'The horse is made ready for battle, but victory rests with the Lord.'"

"Can't that be true in general about making plans? Without bringing God into the equation?"

"Nils, I swear, you're intent on becoming a thorn in my side."

This was a couple weeks after the movie, and the closest thing to a second date after what wasn't really even a first date. She was easy to talk to, but he had trouble seeing her outside the framework of her faith, which seemed to completely envelop her. He had observed her in the snack bar, praying silently, hands folded, before eating her french fries. When he had told her he was mostly raised Catholic, as a way to sort of elevate himself in her eyes, she'd kind of clucked her tongue sympathetically.

"Anyway, I'm going to get my degree and then find a teaching job in the area. I'm not picky, because it'll just be until something opens up in Pembina. As soon as someone moves or retires, I'll be teaching there."

"Or dies?"

"I suppose. But I wouldn't wish for that, of course. Don't get me wrong, I'm not guaranteed a job, but I'm close to people there. My aunt teaches there."

"Why Pembina?"

"That's our original hometown," she'd said, as if it were a fact he should already know. He didn't know much about Pembina, just that it was up north, close to the Canadian border, sort of in the middle of nowhere. She had become more animated, talking about it. "There's a property on the edge of town I've been looking at forever. It's got a lot of trees, and there's enough land to have a little hobby farm, a horse, maybe, some chickens, who knows? But that's where I'd want to raise a family for sure."

"That's a hell of a plan. Sorry. Heck of a plan."

"Well, what's *your* plan?"

"I don't know. Roll through life, taking it as it comes."

She had slapped his arm. "Stop that."

"I guess I'll go to graduate school. A creative writing program."

"Here?"

"I don't know."

"You could be a writer anywhere, couldn't you?"

"Sure. All I need is a typewriter and a post office."

He was afraid she was going to tell him there was a post office in Pembina, but she just smiled and sipped her Orange Julius, and thankfully, they needed to get back to work. Nils doubted if he could ever tell her about what really happened with Kelly, with the Master, the love triangle. He figured Tracy had to be a virgin and would be shocked to learn how often and in how many different positions he and Kelly had done it. Some of what they'd done had not even been enjoyable but seemed important to Kelly to show to him. And he could never tell her about messing around with Kat just minutes after meeting her. *That* had to be some kind of a sin. But maybe he could skip to the part about surviving the wreck. She would no doubt believe that God had picked him up and set him gently down. He didn't think it had anything to do with God. He thought his balance and coordination and reflexes had kicked in automatically. If it had happened without his martial arts training, he might be broken or dead. Or if it happened in the future, when he was weaker and slower, he might be dead.

Now the rain started. He tilted his head back and allowed it to dot his face, soothe his black eye. He stood and slipped onto the screened porch and lay down on the old sofa he used as a summer-time bed and pulled his blanket up. He felt a great satisfaction. He had won the night, every step of the way, like pitching a perfect game and never doubting for a moment that you would. But as soon as he thought this, a hard realization followed: there would probably never be another night on earth like this night. The stars could not line up the same way for him. He didn't need his mother's astrology charts to understand that. And the dumb thing, he thought, would be thinking it was possible and waiting the rest of his life for a night like this to happen again. That would be kind of pathetic.

Maybe he would call Tracy and take her up on her standing of-fer to bring him to church. He didn't really want to go to her church, which was in a strip mall near K-Mart with folding chairs instead of pews. But it would be a way to get to know her. She was someone a person would be able to count on, he thought. She had won a men-tion on the store bulletin board for having the fewest errors in her cash drawer. Maybe they could take a drive up to Pembina and look around, have lunch in some cheerful café where the old ladies would know her by name. She probably wouldn't want to go too far sexually, but he thought he wouldn't mind taking it slow for a change.

A bolt of lightning exploded above the yard and came with a crash of thunder that rattled the old house. Nils flinched, and his heart raced. He thought he could taste the electricity. In a minute, through the window, he saw flames licking up the side of one of the evergreens. The trees were why his father had bought this house; they reminded him of wild Arizona in a town where everything was carefully manicured. Now one was *on fire*. Was it a sign? Wasn't there something in the Bible about a burning bush? But what flashed in his mind next wasn't Tracy's sweet, earnest face. It was Kat, that look in her eyes at the stoplight when she jammed on the gas and burned rubber, that curl in her lip, like she was possessed by something. He knew it wouldn't be good for him, for his soul or otherwise, but he decided he'd go see her when he got up. Bring her some flowers from the neighbor's garden and say, *hey girl, how's it going, what's next?*

This book was set in Maecenas, designed by Michał Jarociński
for Capitalics, Poland's first type foundry.

This book was designed by Shannon Carter, Ian Creeger,
and Gregory Wolfe. It was published in hardcover, paperback,
and electronic formats by Slant Books, Seattle, Washington.

Cover photograph: Wim Wenders, *Abandoned Drive-in, 1983* (detail).
Used with permission.